**"Maybe you need a competition to distract you,"** Quinn challenged.

"What'd you have in mind?" Logan replied.

"A little game of teasing. First one who cracks loses. Or wins," she said. "Depends on how they crack. Scared you can't keep it together? You know what's underneath these clothes and it might be too much temptation for you."

He needed her more than he'd guessed until this very moment. "Oh, I think I'm up to the challenge. What are the rules?"

"Anything goes," she said.

"Fair enough," he said, putting his arm around her waist and lifting her off her feet. He brought his mouth down on hers, kissed her long and deep and shoved the thoughts of everything and everyone else out of his head.

It was just him and Quinn and that big king bed behind him. Win or lose, he knew he needed nothing more than this.

\* \* \*

*The Wedding Dare* by Katherine Garbera
is part of the Destination Wedding series.

D1052262

Dear Reader,

I'm so excited to bring you to Adler and Nick's wedding! There is so much going on and, in each book, a new part of the secret and scandal is revealed. I hope you enjoy this sexy, scandalous ride.

Logan and Quinn have a past and it's not necessarily a bad one. They grew apart as Logan became more obsessed with beating his competitors and taking over as CEO. Quinn is as competitive as Logan is but felt that their relationship was one place they shouldn't be trying to best each other.

Now she's a top reality television producer and on Nantucket to cover his cousin's wedding. His family is falling apart as more secrets from his parents are revealed, and Logan turns to her for comfort and distraction. Quinn tells herself that they are hooking up for old time's sake but her heart isn't so sure. As much as Logan has changed, she's not sure she can trust him.

I love a summer wedding and getting to be on Nantucket with its beaches was so much fun.

Also, as this is my twenty-fifth year writing for Harlequin Desire, I want to say thank you for reading my books.

Happy reading!

*Katherine*

# KATHERINE GARBERA

—

## THE WEDDING DARE

HARLEQUIN
DESIRE

Thanks as always to my brilliant editor, Charles, who always sees what I'm trying to do and how to make it better!

Recycling programs for this product may not exist in your area.

ISBN-13: 978-1-335-73551-5

The Wedding Dare

Copyright © 2022 by Katherine Garbera

This edition published by arrangement with Harlequin Books S.A.

For questions and comments about the quality of this book, please contact us at CustomerService@Harlequin.com.

Harlequin Enterprises ULC
22 Adelaide St. West, 41st Floor
Toronto, Ontario M5H 4E3, Canada
www.Harlequin.com

Printed in U.S.A.

**Katherine Garbera** is the *USA TODAY* bestselling author of more than ninety-five books. Her writing is known for its emotional punch and sizzling sensuality. She lives in the Midlands of the UK with the love of her life; her son, who recently graduated university; and a spoiled miniature dachshund. You can find her online at www.katherinegarbera.com and on Facebook, Twitter and Instagram.

Visit her Author Profile page at Harlequin.com, or katherinegarbera.com, for more titles.

You can also find Katherine Garbera on Facebook, along with other Harlequin Desire authors, at Facebook.com/harlequindesireauthors!

For Georgina Mogg.
Our entire family got lucky when Lucas met you.
Thanks for all the laughs and good times.
I'm looking forward for more to come.

# One

Sunshine and blue skies. It was the kind of June day that made most people happy to be on Nantucket. But Logan knew the cell phone signal would be iffy at best and that he was on the island to attend the wedding of his business rival. Not exactly his idea of fun.

And having arrived at his grandmother's large "cottage" on Nantucket to find his brothers all gathered in the study secretly conferring instead of socializing with other wedding guests, Logan couldn't help but hope that it meant his cousin Adler had come to her senses and jilted Nick Williams.

His family was large and the connections were complex but they were all here on Nantucket for the wedding of his cousin Adler Osborn. Adler's father was the rock star Toby Osborn and her mom was Logan's aunt Musette, who had died when Adler was a baby. His mom had been a surrogate mother for Adler and honestly his cousin was more like a sister to them all.

Nick Williams was another story. For as long as Logan could remember Nick and his father, Tad Williams, had been rivals to Bisset Industries. Logan had probably spent more time with Nick than any of his siblings and personally couldn't stand the guy, who was always trying to outmaneuver him.

In fact, Logan had been late arriving on Nantucket because he'd wanted to one-up Nick and had been negotiating to buy a patent out from under him.

"What's going on?" he asked his brother Zac, who'd been on the island for several days with his new girlfriend and the maid of honor at the wedding, Iris Collins.

"Dad's just admitted to having an affair with Cora Williams thirty-five years ago. Nick is our half brother," Zac informed Logan as he handed him a whiskey and Coke.

"Are you f-ing kidding me?" he said. Not the news he was hoping for. Maybe he'd heard Zac wrong.

Logan didn't need another brother. He already had three—besides his younger brother Zac, there was Leo—also younger—who had left Bisset Industries and started his own successful company after butt-ing heads with Logan. Then there was their eldest brother, Dare, who was a United States Senator. And their little sister, Mari, who was engaged to the Formula One driver Inigo Velasquez.

"I wish I was. Mom is…well, very upset. Cora and her husband are with her and Dad in the study, with Carlton," Dare said, pouring more whiskey into his own glass and offering more to Zac and Leo as well.

"Am I the last to learn?" he asked. He wasn't surprised that his dad had brought in Carlton Mansford—the family PR person and his father's assistant.

"Mari's not here yet," Leo said, mentioning their youngest sibling and only sister. "But she is on the ferry. I texted her the deets."

"The deets?"

"Stop acting like you don't know what it means," Leo said.

"I just prefer it when we talk like we're adults," Logan said, feeling angry and spoiling for a fight.

"Thanks, Dad Junior, should we expect any surprises from you too?" Leo asked.

Logan lunged for his brother, fists clenched. He could use a fight; it would give him something to do with all the anger welling up inside him at the thought of Nick Williams being their brother.

"Stop it," Dare said, wrapping his arm around Logan and physically hauling him back. "Us fighting is the last thing Mom needs right now."

"You're right," Logan said, pushing away from

Dare and looking out the window at the neatly man-
icured gardens that spread toward the ocean in the
distance.

*Family.*

It was the one thing that had made him the man he
was, but it was also the most difficult thing for him to
navigate. Logan took pride when people said he had
his father's tenacity and his mother's charm. Argu-
ably, he was the best blend of his parents. Though he
knew that Leo might argue, but his youngest brother
just liked to debate. And Dare would argue there
weren't any good qualities in their father, a senti-
ment shared by Zac. Marielle adored their father, so
she'd side with him.

"How is Mom?" Dare asked.

Only Zac had been in the conservatory when the
news about their father's affair had been revealed.

"She looked broken," Zac said. "I didn't want to
let her be alone with Dad, but he wasn't going without her."

"He won't hurt her," Logan said. "He would never
do that."

"Well, other than sleeping with another woman
while Mom was pregnant with you and then finding
out thirty some odd years later that her niece's fiancé is really our half brother," Zac said sardonically.

"Right. Aside from that," Logan said. "This isn't
like Dad."

"It's exactly like Dad," Leo said. "You just don't see it because you want to be like him."

"I don't want to be like him, I am like him," Logan said.

"At least the good parts," Zac said.

Dare snickered under his breath. "I've seen him at the negotiating table, Z, he's got some of Dad's tougher qualities too."

"So? I pair it with Mom's charm," Logan said.

"Or try to," Leo added.

"Are you looking for a fight?" Logan asked.

"Yes. I'm not you. I can't go out there and be all broody, I have to be the one who's smiling and friendly. But I don't want Nick Williams as a brother. The man has a reputation that's almost as bad as yours, Logan."

"Now we know why," Dare said. "He's a victim just like us. From what Zac said, Nick seemed blind-sided by the announcement too."

"This is a complete cluster f—"

"Watch your language, boys. There's a lady in the room," Mari called out as she entered. Their sister wore her blond hair flowing past her shoulders to the middle of her back. She looked like she'd just stepped off the runway at Fashion Week instead of the ferry, and the smile on her face was genuine and not forced the way it used to be before she'd fallen in love with Inigo Velasquez.

Everyone turned to greet and hug her. Logan went

last. He and Mari had always been close due to their relationship with their father.

"So, Dad did it again," Mari said. "I knew that affair he got busted for before I was born couldn't have been the only one."

"Yeah, so what are we going to do about Nick?" Dare asked. "Carlton and Mom and Dad will deal with the outside world."

"I had dinner with Nick the other night. I'll be the one to feel him out and see what he wants," Zac said.

Yeah, of course, they'd have to see what Nick wanted.

Logan had arrived on Nantucket prepared to play nice all weekend with his business rival and archenemy Nick Williams. Only because the bastard was marrying Logan's cousin by marriage, Adler Osborn. She was his mom's only niece. Adler's mother had died when she was a toddler—and his mom had assumed the role of mother to her. He adored his cousin, but thought she had horrid taste in men.

He was still reflecting on her horrid taste in men three hours later in the bar at the hotel. The wedding guests were gathering on the beach for a clambake with all the wedding attendees for the weekend's festivities. Apparently, the wedding was still on. Logan sat sullenly in the bar—he could admit when he was being a brat—until he saw Quinn Murray walk through the lobby.

His college lover—and the producer in charge of

filming Adler's celebrity wedding for a television network. He hadn't expected to feel anything when he saw her. But there she was walking through the hotel like she owned the place. There was no mistaking her long red hair and her brown eyes, which had a way of boring past the bullshit he used to charm most people to the truth beneath his comments. And of course, that petite, curvy body of hers that no matter how many lovers there had been since they'd been a couple, he couldn't forget.

She was the one woman he'd never been able to charm or figure out. There was something about her that mesmerized him. And he hated that. He prided himself on seeing a problem and solving it. And tonight, when his entire world was off its axis, he could use the distraction that Quinn would provide.

He wasn't kidding himself that she'd fall back into bed with him—that wasn't Quinn's way—but she'd give him the distraction he needed. He told the bartender to put his drinks on his tab and followed her out into the summer evening.

Quinn was already on the path that led down to the shore, moving quickly, as if in a hurry. When wasn't she? She was just as ambitious as he was and had never let anything throw her off her path—even their brief love affair. She'd said he was too driven for her, but she had always had the same drive.

When he got to the beach, Zac and Nick were drunkenly singing and looking over at Adler and Iris.

The last thing Logan wanted to do was get to know his new half sibling. He and Nick were business rivals of the worst kind, both always trying to one-up the other. Zac had somehow come back from Australia, where he'd been training for the America's Cup to start his own team and raise money to fund his next Cup run, and, in the course of a week, managed to start dating Iris, who was smart, sophisticated, and seemed to enthrall his normally free-spirited brother. He shook his head.

The Nick thing.

How the hell was he going to be cordial to a man whose business he was planning to undercut? How the hell was he going to convince everyone that he'd put those plans in motion a long time ago and that they couldn't be stopped? How the hell—

"So, you've got a new brother," Quinn said, breaking into his thoughts. "That must have thrown you for about half a second."

He glanced over at her. In the shadowy light from the clambake he could barely make out the freckles that dotted the bridge of her nose and her cheeks.

"Yeah, not what I was expecting to deal with today," he said acerbically.

"I figured. You probably were coming in all magnanimous and then—wham! Your enemy is actually your brother."

"Is there a point to all of this, Quinn?"

"Nah, just seeing if you are rattled or ticked or

have already figured this out and made a plan to manage it," she said. "Plus, you looked a bit like Heathcliff staring broodingly over at Nick and Zac."

"You like Heathcliff," he said. She liked books with angst and drama in them.

"Not my point. You okay?" she asked, sitting next to him on one of the chairs the hotel had provided.

He looked over at her. It had been years since he'd let anyone close to him. He had his brothers and sister, and sometimes he relied on his assistant, but most of the time he kept his own counsel and he liked it that way.

"Yeah."

She arched one eyebrow at him. "That didn't even sound real."

"It didn't? I thought it was convincing," he said.

"I don't buy it," she said, reaching over and putting her hand on top of his. A zing went straight through his body and right to his groin. He straightened his legs. He'd wanted to be distracted from his own internal debate about this new brother he didn't want. But he knew that Quinn was complicated. It was okay to be turned on by her. She was hot as hell and they'd always had this kind of reaction to each other.

But that was it. She was complex and real to him. She wasn't a woman he'd picked up in a bar and could take back to his room for one night. He liked Quinn, respected her, and she was very good friends with the women in his family. He knew this couldn't go anywhere, but that didn't stop him from turning his hand over and running his finger along her wrist and up her arm.

She shivered and leaned in closer to him. She still wore that faint vanilla scent that always made him think of her. She tipped her head to the side, studying him. He wasn't sure what she'd see, but he knew that tonight he didn't want her realism. He needed to believe the image he always presented to the world.

So he leaned in slowly to see if she'd allow him to kiss her, and she licked her lips, putting her hand on the side of his jaw, her fingers moving along the side of his neck before she squeezed his shoulder as she came closer to her.

Her lips brushed his and he pushed aside all of the worries of the day and took the kiss he hadn't realized he'd been missing for ten long years. Her mouth opened under his and he forgot about complications and messed-up family relationships. He forgot about the wedding and the merger he'd already set in motion. He forgot about everything except Quinn Murray and the fact that she kissed him the way she did everything else in life. With passion and need. And she made him realize how busy he'd been with his business life and how he'd neglected this side of himself.

But this was Quinn Murray. The one woman he'd never been able to resist. He needed a distraction, so he lifted her out of her chair and onto his lap to deepen the kiss. She pushed both hands into his hair, holding him close to her. He had found the distraction he was looking for in the fire of her kiss and knew that, for tonight at least, he didn't need to figure out anything other than pleasing this woman.

*Logan.* He'd always been the one problem she'd never been able to solve. The one guy she couldn't just leave in the past. He was hot, anyone could see that, with his dirty-blond hair, chiseled jaw and ice-blue eyes. He'd always had striking looks. He was muscled because he had an amazing amount of energy. She knew from his sister, Marielle, that he still got up every day at five to work out and then went into the office, staying until almost midnight.

When they'd been in college, it had been attractive to be with a man who was so driven, so determined to succeed, but then she'd realized that he'd never stop competing with her over everything. And she'd liked the challenge at first. But soon it was more than who got the better grades, it was…well, everything, and when she started to realize that no prize was ever going to be enough for him, she'd walked away. But a part of her, the part that had her climbing all over his lap like it had been nine months since she'd made love to anything other than her vibrator…well, she wanted him. Even if it was just because of the long weekend they were both spending in Nantucket.

He tasted good. *Addictive*. She had to be honest and say he was the best man she'd ever kissed. There was something unhurried and yet raw and sensual about the way he kissed her. He took his time, but she felt completely laid bare by it. The passion between them hadn't waned in the years they'd been apart and, as much as she wished it had, she was glad it hadn't.

She liked being in his arms, feeling his hard-on under her hip and his hands roaming up and down her back.

Quinn knew that this wasn't real. She didn't kid herself that it was anything more than Logan distracting himself from finding out that a man he considered his rival and enemy was now his brother. But that didn't mean he hadn't turned her on.

She broke the kiss and opened her eyes to find herself looking into that icy-blue stare of his. The honesty there, the unfettered need, struck a chord deep within her. She'd always been able to see past the ego and the arrogance that he wore like a haughty cloak. But tonight, what she saw there mirrored what she wanted.

They needed this night. They'd never really had any closure, and this could be it. Just a night of burning up the sheets and, in the morning, he'd go back to the mess that his family was and she'd go to work producing *Adler's Destination Wedding* for the television network she worked for.

"That was unexpected," she said.

"Unwelcome?" he asked. "I know we broke up a long time ago, but I have to be honest, Ace, every time I see you, I think about kissing you."

Ace.

He was the only one who called her that. It had been years since she'd heard him use the nickname, though.

"I think about it sometimes too," she admitted.

"But not more than me, right?" he asked. "I know I was too much at the end and, hell, I probably still am..."

It was there in the way he paused. He wanted to hook up, but he didn't want to appear to be the one to suggest it in case she said no. This was why their relationship hadn't worked. Quinn believed with her entire heart that when she found a man to spend the rest of her life with, she'd feel comfortable being vulnerable to him. But with Logan she'd had to keep her guard up. He was always competing, always trying to win, and after a while she'd realized she couldn't compete all the time.

"That kiss was hot and a nice trip down memory lane," she said. "But I don't think either of us need the complications a hookup would bring."

"Does it have to be complicated?" he asked.

"I'm not sure, but you are hedging like you can't admit you want me, and I'm way past that," she said. Turning thirty had burned away a lot of the artifice she'd used in the past. "I'm not interested in being your dirty little secret."

"It wouldn't have to be a secret," he said. "I don't mind if it's a little dirty."

A shiver went through her and she knew she didn't mind if it was dirty either. The thing about Logan was that once he committed to something, he never backed down. Maybe commitment was the wrong word, because the only thing he was dedicated to was his career.

"Why me?" she asked. "There're tons of women here you could hook up with."

"Sometimes I wake up in a sweat thinking about you and me together. I know we don't work for more than a few nights, but I still want you, Ace. I always have. And I'm not sure I have the strength to deny myself tonight. I'm not trying to push you into anything. If you say no, I'll let you walk away. But I'm praying you'll say yes because, after this day, I need you."

He needed her.

Was there a more powerful aphrodisiac in the world?

For other women, maybe, but having a man like Logan need her was all it took to crack her resolve and make her want to give in to the cravings that had been awakened the moment she'd seen him tonight. He was strong—a titan of industry. A man who left nothing but gobbled-up companies and bemused people who weren't sure how they could like a man who was so arrogant. But tonight, Logan Bisset, who had never needed anything or anyone, needed her.

And she needed him too.

Needed to remember what it was like to be in his arms and forget about competitions and standing on her own.

She stood and held her hand out to him. He looked at her, those ice-blue eyes hard to read in the flickering light of the bonfire. But his hand when it engulfed hers was warm and he tugged her slightly off balance and into his arms. She inhaled the scent of his spicy aftershave and closed her eyes, hoping she wasn't making the biggest mistake of her life.

# Two

She smelled of summer and sunshine and something pure. Quinn was the kind of distraction he longed for. She was familiar. She knew his faults better than anyone and she had no expectations from him. He tugged her back down onto his lap.

He lowered his mouth to kiss her, but she put her hand on his lips. A tingle went straight through to his groin and he groaned.

"What?"

"Are you sure about this?" she asked. "I mean I know you—"

"Do you?" he countered. The last thing—the very last thing—he wanted to do was to talk. He wanted her to just be some hot lay so he could forget. But when had Quinn ever been that?

He had the feeling that he was on the cusp of making a big mistake. But then everything he'd ever thought he knew about his life had changed. His enemy—he knew that made him sound like Machiavelli but didn't give a crap—was now his half brother. Everyone was going to expect him to make nicey-nice, except he'd already put in motion a plan to crush Nick and his family's company, Williams, Inc.

Quinn shifted on his lap, settling closer to his chest and rubbing her finger over his lips. "Talking about it will help."

"I don't think so, Quinn. I can't. I can screw. I can drink. But I don't want to talk."

"You're being a douchebag, Logan."

"It's kind of my thing," he said, not at all joking. He looked into Quinn's brown eyes and realized that he was seconds away from spending this night alone, listening to his younger brother Zac sing off-key lyrics about love, and stewing in his own ruthlessness.

She sighed.

He was losing her. He put his hand lightly on her thigh and took a deep breath. "I don't want you to think I'm easy."

She threw her head back and laughed. She laughed so hard and loud, her entire body shook with it, and he smiled himself because he'd been the cause. After a day filled with anger and uncertainty, he needed this.

He needed her.

Damn.

Only for tonight, he promised himself.

He was Logan Bisset. He didn't need anyone. Especially a curvy, determined redhead who had always beaten him at his own game. But then she turned, putting her hands on his shoulders and straddling him on the beach lounger.

She lowered her head, the sides of her hair swinging forward to brush against his cheek a moment before her lips brushed over his. Her breath was sweet-smelling and warm, and he put his hands on her hips to hold her to him just in case she changed her mind and decided to leave.

She tipped her head to the side, deepening the kiss, her tongue thrusting into his mouth. He groaned as he felt his erection growing, exercising every amount of control he could muster to keep from rubbing it against her. He knew she didn't want to go to bed with him. And he respected her and wouldn't push. But he hadn't really had a kiss like this in too long.

He avoided women like Quinn, who could make him feel as well as turn him on. It was easier to just hook up. But tonight when he felt like he was shattered and knew that the worst of the fallout over the Nick situation wasn't over due to his own actions in stealing a patent out from under Williams, Inc., he needed this. Needed her.

She pulled back, sitting on his thighs.

Their eyes met and he saw compassion in her gaze. It was probably one of the things that made her so successful at her job. She was driven and competitive, but she also had empathy, which he knew he lacked.

*Please*, he thought, *don't ask me anything else.*

"Is it a whiskey or beer night?"

"I was thinking serious drinking," he admitted.

"Whiskey then. I think there is a bar set up down at the clambake. Want to go grab some food and drinks?"

No. But he knew that if he said he wanted to go back to his room, she'd leave.

"Sure. But I'm not going to be socializing."

"Duh," she said with a wink as she hopped off his lap. "When are you ever?"

He shook his head as she held her hand out to him. He stood and took her hand. She linked their fingers together and then looked up at him. "Don't think this is more than friendship."

He nodded. They had always been like oil and water and he was pretty sure that would never change. "Why are you doing this?"

"You need a friend tonight. Someone you can let go and be yourself with, and you can't with your family right now," she said.

"Thank you," he said.

"Don't thank me yet. We still have to navigate the clambake," she warned.

Where his entire extended family and a bunch of friends of his parents' and cousin, whom he'd known his entire life, were. Only the inner circle of his family and the Williams' siblings knew the truth about Nick.

He could bullshit and keep secrets with the best of them. But he'd never been good at hiding his emotions. When he was mad, everyone knew it. He doubted that was going to change tonight. But as they approached the bonfire, his brother had given up singing and now Adler's father, the rocker Toby Osborn, was singing his number-one hit song about rebellion and making his own path. Logan, who had always been the model Bisset son, listened to the lyrics. *My path could have been easier if I had been a different man.* Damn but those words resonated. He shook off that thought as he just followed Quinn.

Logan went to the bar, ordered two Jack and Coke, and then turned and bumped into Nick Williams. The groom, his business rival and, as of today, his half brother. The other man's eyes were bloodshot, and he looked…well, like Logan felt. Nick had the worst of the news and if Logan were a better man, he would have tried to comfort him. But at the end of the day, Logan was still himself.

"Fuck," Nick said. "Of course, I bump into you."

"Ditto," Logan said.

Nick gave a little half smile. "The only silver lining to this entire shit storm is the fact that I know you hate it as much as I do."

Logan fought to keep from smiling. He'd never spent any time with Nick other than on the other side of a boardroom table negotiating to outbid him. Now he regretted it. There was something familiar in the other man; probably that DNA his father had contributed.

"Exactly my thought," Logan admitted. "Let me buy you a drink."

"Like hell," Nick said. "I'll buy the drinks."

"You're buying them all," Logan pointed out gently. "This is your event. Where is your bride?"

"Listening to her dad sing," Nick said, shaking himself and then standing taller. "And waiting for her drink. So move it, Bisset. I don't want to keep her waiting."

"You say Bisset like it's a curse but you—"

"Don't. Don't say it out loud. I'm not ready to hear it, especially from you," Nick said. He pushed Logan out of the way and Logan let himself be moved.

As hard as this was for him, it had to be at least the same if not more so for Nick. The family had gathered for his wedding and on the eve of everyone they knew arriving on an island, he'd learned he was the biological son of his business rival and the

man who'd raised his worst enemy. Logan just nodded and turned to go find Quinn.

He knew that over the next few days things would
more than likely get worse as the news broke in the
press, despite Carlton's best public relations spin.
And at some point, Logan realized, he was going to
have to come clean with his dad and with Nick about
the patent he'd purchased out from under him after
Nick had beaten him to the punch on another deal
three months earlier.

Damn.

Quinn danced in the moonlight near his sister, Iris
Collins and Adler. Logan stood there in the shadows wanting to join the women but also knowing
he should let them be. Let Quinn help Adler adjust
to the news that was rattling her as well. His cousin
had been born into a world of paparazzi and tabloid
headlines. Her mother had been the younger lover
of a famous rock star known for his debauched lifestyle. Then, when Adler was two, her mom had died
of a drug overdose, which had simply fanned interest
in her. All of Adler's life, she'd been struggling to
stay out of the spotlight but televising this wedding
was the kind of media attention Adler wanted. The
kind that would give her legitimacy and take away
the tabloid headlines—until today.

Until her very respectable fiancé turned out to
be the bastard—was that a word that anyone used

anymore?—son of a business rival. How fucked up was that?

He had to wonder sometimes if fate was just having a massive laugh at his entire family. His dad had certainly stirred up some bad karma in the business world over the way he stabbed associates in the back and undercut rivals. And, of course, in his personal life he'd slept around on his wife, had affairs and lied to them all.

Was he any better? Logan wondered. He tried to be the charming and kind person that his mother was. Tried hard to balance his ruthlessness with a softer side, but it wasn't all that easy.

"Dude, you're bringing me down by standing in the shadows and brooding," Leo said, coming over and taking one of the drinks from his hand. "It's a party. Even a workaholic like you should know what that is."

"That drink was for someone else," Logan said, taking a swallow of his own. At least Leo would prove a distraction. His youngest brother and he had always been competitive with each other. If Leo had been born earlier, closer to his own age, Logan had often thought that Leo would have challenged him for the CEO position of the family company. Instead he'd struck out on his own and created a business that was quickly expanding.

"No one was going to want to drink with you until you lost that dour expression," Leo said.

"You are so annoying," Logan responded. "Why are you such a little prick all the time?"

Leo raised his eyebrows at him. "Because you're such a big one. Everyone else gives you leave to be an ass, but since I'm a lot like you, I know better than to feed that need. You need someone to cut you down."

He smiled. "As do you. You know there's a company I've been hearing about that does American-made leather goods that's gunning for your market share."

"That little Etsy shop owner?" he asked.

Logan nodded. Danni Eldridge was making all sorts of waves in the business community and one of the board members at Bisset Industries had forwarded Logan a prospectus recommending they invest in her company. He'd turned it down. They weren't going to buy a company that would put them in direct competition with Leo and his niche of the leather goods market. Leo's company had started out small and his online presence had grown it into a multi-million-dollar business.

"Danni Eldridge is a fad. I know because I grew my business from Instagram followers by showing consumers a lifestyle they wanted. It takes a lot of acumen, determination and drive to turn that into a real business. I don't think she'll last," Leo said.

"Fair enough," Logan said.

"I thought you were getting drinks for both of us," Quinn said, coming up to them.

"I stole yours," Leo said. "I'll grab you a fresh one."

As Leo turned away and left, Quinn grabbed Logan's hand, pulling him toward the bonfire. "Dance with me?"

"Yes."

Quinn had noticed Logan talking to his brother. Given Logan's mood tonight, and the fact that Mari had mentioned they'd almost had a fist fight earlier, she thought it would be a good idea to interrupt. And she was glad she had. Dancing with Logan was almost as good as sex. And about a thousand times safer for her heart and soul.

Or so she'd thought until Toby and his band slowed things down with the ballad that everyone said he'd written for Adler's mom after she'd died. It was the love song he'd never written when she was alive, and it spoke of love and longing. It was a sensual bluesy-sounding song that had Quinn pulling Logan into her arms and closing her eyes.

His hands fell naturally to her hips and he pulled her close enough that she felt the brush of his chest against her breasts as she twined her arms around his neck. It had been over three years since she'd danced with anyone. She just felt like she was too old to go clubbing. That had to be the reason why every touch of Logan's hand was sending tingles all through her body.

His legs brushed against hers. Since it was hot

and summery, she'd dressed in a flirty little sundress instead of her typical khakis, so she felt the
brush of his thigh against her bare skin. He wore a
pair of Bermuda shorts, so it wasn't skin-on-skin—
thank God for that.

He swayed with her to the music, their bodies
finding a natural rhythm, the one they'd always had.
No matter how out of sync they'd been emotionally,
physically they'd always just had this link. This bond
that had been hard to shatter and break.

Quinn knew that a smart woman would turn and
walk away. Go back to her hotel room and work or
do something else—anything else. But under the
full summer moon, she didn't want to do the smart
thing. Her entire life had been about following the
practical path and, for this one night, she knew she
wanted to be impulsive.

To follow her hormones or her lust-filled self and
indulge in everything Logan was offering. Just pretend that she could sleep with him and walk away
unscarred even though deep inside— *Shut up.* She
pushed the logical, thinking part of herself to the
back of her mind.

She wanted something fun to remember about
this night, a night when the people she loved were
hurting and struggling to make sense of something
that was hard to wrap their heads around. But then,
August Bisset had always thought he was above the

rules everyone else followed and he'd never really worried about those he wounded with his actions.

Her eyes met Logan's and she saw the hurt and pain in his eyes, the need and want as well. He didn't want to talk, and that said everything. He wasn't processing this at all; he needed to forget and she needed to remember. She wanted a night of passion without the pain that had always followed when they'd been a couple in college. She wanted a night that could just be about this feeling of rightness they'd always had physically.

And she was going to take it.

She didn't care if she regretted it the next day or if there were consequences. She'd deal with them. She would have regrets either way.

She pulled his head down to hers and kissed him. Not the tentative way she had earlier on the beach chair, but in a way that said *Take me. Take me now.* She undulated against him in time to the music and it took Logan a split second before he reciprocated.

His tongue tangled with hers as his hands cupped her butt and lifted her more fully into his body. They danced until the music stopped and then Logan raised his head and looked down at her.

The questions in his eyes weren't ones she wanted to answer. But she hadn't exactly said yes earlier and he didn't want to read her wrong again. He needed to hear the words.

"Walk with me on the beach?" she asked. "Let's go somewhere where we can be alone."

"Only if you're sure," he said. "I don't need something else to regret tomorrow."

"I don't want to be something you regret," she answered. "I want you, Logan. No strings. Nothing but the summer night and this moment."

"Me too," he said.

He slipped his hand in hers and led her away from the bonfire, stopping to grab a blanket from the pile the hotel staff had set out for the guests. They walked away from the crowd and the music. The night got darker and the breeze a bit stronger, but she grew more confident.

For too long she'd ignored the fact that she'd never had the closure she'd wanted with Logan. She'd given him an ultimatum—stop turning everything into a competition or leave—their senior year of college and had expected that he'd give in to her. Instead he'd walked away. She hadn't had a chance to end things the way she'd wanted.

And this, of course, wasn't an ending but it was one last time in his arms so she'd be able to finally put that chapter of her life to rest. Mark it ended and move on from Logan Bisset once and for all. It was past time that she did it, and tonight seemed the right moment.

A moment when they could just be Logan and Quinn and forget about the rest of the world.

# Three

The farther away they got from the bonfire, the more relaxed Logan seemed to be. It was as if, in the darkness, with only the moon to light their way, he could let down his guard. A part of Quinn, the part that, if she were honest, probably still loved him a little bit, softened. She had always thought that Logan's biggest problem was the fact that he thought he had to be invincible. She knew he'd never change. There was too much August Bisset in him for that to happen.

The walk gave her time to think. The thing about Logan was that he was better to deal with as an impulse and then move on. As soon as she started worrying about his happiness—seeing the broken man she wanted to fix no matter that she knew she couldn't—she should walk away.

For her own sanity.

He stopped and let the blanket drop to the sand at their feet, pulling her into his arms with his chest to her back, just holding her.

"I'll deny it if you ever repeat this, but there are times when I agree with Zac. I totally understand his love of the sea. There's something soothing about the ocean that tempts me to forget all my problems," he said. His voice was a low rumble and there was a softness to his words that surprised her.

This wasn't the Logan she'd dated in college; she'd do well to remember that. And it was a good and bad thing, she thought.

"Why wouldn't you want anyone to know that?" she asked, putting her hands over his wrists where they crossed over her stomach.

"Because I'm always giving Zac a hard time about being a sailor. I mean I know he's so much more than that, as he is a captain for the America's Cup and it's highly competitive and he's very good at it. But he's my little brother…"

She shook her head. As an only child, she'd never really understood the sibling dynamic—especially the Bisset siblings—but she knew that whatever it was meant a lot to all of them. "Well, I doubt I'll have a chance to speak to him, so your secret is safe with me."

He sighed then.

"What?"

"Why is it that you're the one woman I can trust?" he asked.

"I don't know," she admitted. "I think if we dwell on this, then we will be heading back to the bonfire."

He moved to stand next to her. They were facing the inky-dark ocean and the gentle sound of the waves wasn't as soothing as it had been a few moments ago. This was what she'd hoped to avoid. There was no closure in talking to Logan. He was always going to be the guy he'd been. He was always going to let her down, not through a fault in him—he could only be the man he was—but in her own expectation of the man she wanted him to be.

"That would be the safe choice," he said. "But I've never been one to avoid a risk and if you are anything like the woman I used to know, you're the same."

She groaned.

He laughed.

She shrugged. "I'm not that woman anymore, Logan."

"Sure you are, Ace. That's why you're standing with me down the beach from the crowd. And if you are anything like me, you remember how good we were together," he said.

They had been good together. Physically they'd always had that spark. There was something in him that drew her like a moth to a flame, ignoring the danger for the chance to get closer to him for a short amount of time. She wanted to turn and walk away. She was thirty. Smarter now than she had ever been. Well, if not smarter, at least wiser.

Wiser.

What a dumb thought. She wanted Logan and was trying to justify it, but no matter what she did tonight—walk away or stay—she'd have regrets in the morning. The only difference would be what she regretted.

He bent and straightened the blanket, sitting on it and looking up at her as he pulled a bottle of Jack Daniel's from his pocket. "Drink?"

She almost shook her head and left.

Wiser.

Instead she sat next to him. He'd sit there by himself and drink the entire bottle and, as much as she knew she should probably leave, she couldn't let him do it. Plus, it had been a long time since they'd been this close, and she wanted him. She'd forgotten the potency of his appeal when they were apart, living their own lives.

But up close with his bright, light blue eyes and strong, square jaw that she knew was a harbinger of his stubbornness, she couldn't resist him. She couldn't even pretend that she was going to leave the beach without having him. But she promised herself she was doing it on her own terms. Not his.

This was for her.

Quinn snatched the bottle from him and took a drink. She loved whiskey, which was why she resisted drinking it whenever she could. But it felt right tonight. She leaned back on her elbows after she handed the bottle over to him.

"The night sky on Nantucket always seems bigger and brighter to me. Especially out here. I remember the first time I visited…"

"I do too. You were so nervous to meet Gran and she immediately fell in love with you when you sided with her," Logan said.

She smiled. Logan was used to bullying his way through life but his grandmother, though she loved him, wouldn't have any of it. The two women had bonded over not taking Logan's bullshit. That relationship was one of the things she'd missed when they'd broken up.

"Gran still thinks the world of you," Logan said, as if reading her thoughts. "She'd love to see you."

That was nice to know, but was there anything worse than an ex-girlfriend who didn't move on? "We're not a couple."

"I know. I guess that's why we are talking and drinking instead of hooking up."

"Definitely."

Talking and drinking.

It wasn't what he wanted to do. He wanted dirty, mind-numbing sex. But he wasn't interested in going back and finding another woman. He wanted it with Quinn. Only Quinn.

And she wanted to talk.

"What's it like to work in television?" he asked, going along with her wishes. "I thought you wanted to direct movies and be the next Kathryn Bigelow."

She took a sip of the Jack instead of answering.

"I thought you wanted to talk," he said gently.

He had the feeling she wanted him to talk. He wasn't going to. Maybe he'd feel like discussing this new half brother when he was dead, but probably not any time before that.

"I did. I do. That's a complicated question. So TV… I like it. It's pretty exciting doing destination weddings. There are always a million things that don't go to plan, but it keeps me on my toes. And I have a travel series on YouTube…kind of a side hustle."

He hadn't realized she was a YouTuber. "Does producing not pay enough?"

"No, why?"

"You said 'side hustle.'"

"Yeah, I don't know. Seems like everyone has one now and I figured it was a way to monetize my downtime."

He looked over at her. "You know a lot of people in my life give me crap for being a workaholic, but you pretty much just admitted to being one."

"When you look at it that way, I guess, but the

thing is, I'm at these really great locations and I sort of explore them with my drone camera and then do a voice-over… I know it sounds like work, but it gives me the freedom to create my own content, which is what I originally wanted to do. TV pays the bills, the YouTube stuff lets me make little mini documentaries. Does that make any sense?"

It sort of did. It was so like Quinn to be practical about taking her degree and using it, at the same time finding a rewarding way to fulfill her dreams. He envied her. She'd even made working all the time sound balanced and fulfilling. The one thing he'd never been able to achieve.

He shoved his hands into his hair and looked up at the starry night. His mind was a beehive of activity and the one thing he'd hoped to calm it wasn't working. He could smell her perfume drifting to him each time the breeze shifted in his direction. If he rolled over, he could touch her, they were sitting so close on the blanket. But she wanted to talk.

And talking was making it worse, reminding him of all he'd chosen to walk away from. Would he be a different man if they'd stayed together? Duh, right? But would he be any happier? Frankly, in his mind—

"What are you thinking?" she asked.

"Just about if you would have made my life better or if I would have ruined yours had we stayed together," he said, honestly.

"Logan, don't do that. We aren't the kind of couple

who are meant for anything but competing. We're really good at putting together the best debate and then trouncing each other. Or making everything into a game... you know it and I know it."

"I do. It's just when you talk, I'm tempted to let myself believe I could be a better man."

"You're a good man," she said. "This isn't like you. Why do you think you need to be better?"

"No reason," he said. "Just the thing with Nick and Dad is throwing me."

*Yeah, right*, his conscience jeered. Like he hadn't spent the last few months plotting to dismantle everything Nick Williams had built over the last few years. As if he wasn't a vindictive man who had lost one too many times, so he'd gone for the jugular and now...now he knew that when what he'd done to take Nick down came out, his father's extramarital affair was going to pale in comparison.

"You okay?" she asked. "When I said talk and drink, I thought we could do something fun."

"Like what?" he asked.

"Find out what we'd been up to since the last time we chatted," she said.

"Like a girl's brunch?"

She punched him in the shoulder, and it was harder than he'd expected.

"No, asshole. Like two friends catching up."

He reached over and squeezed her hand. "I'd like

that. Tell me about the videos you make. How did that start?"

She groaned.

"What?"

"You won't like the answer," she warned him.

"It's my night for not liking things," he said. Honestly, there wasn't anything she could say that would hurt more than knowing he was going to drive a wedge in his family that would make welcoming his new half brother impossible.

"It started after you and I broke up. I took a job on one of those catamaran cruise tours and worked my way around the Caribbean."

"Why wouldn't I like that?" he asked.

"Because I went with Cruz," she said.

She was right. He didn't like it. Cruz and he had competed for everything in college, including Quinn. Of course the other man would have made a play for her when they'd broken up. "We weren't together anymore."

"I know. That's why I went with him," she said. "Not my best moment. But Cruz guessed that's why I'd said yes. He actually is a really decent guy. We had fun and he suggested I do travel videos."

"It was a good suggestion. I'm glad something came out of our breakup."

"Me too. Mainly, that's why I'm afraid to hook up now," she said. "It wasn't easy getting over you, Logan."

"You broke up with me," he reminded her.

"Only because I knew you'd never stop competing with me. I know it sounds silly but that morning you suggested we see who could get their Starbucks order first was it. Then when we got back, you were trying to tell me that our latest exam results, which were the same, weren't really and you had done a longer essay so essentially you'd won. Well, I realized it would never be enough for you to tie with me. You have to be number one," she said.

"What's wrong with that?" he asked.

"Nothing, but I wanted something different."

Something he couldn't deliver. So instead of sex with him, she was talking, and it wasn't going to get either of them what they wanted.

He should leave. Just get up and go.

When he rolled to his side to do so, she stopped him.

Quinn tugged Logan down next to her on the blanket and rolled so she was facing him. He was complex and always made her...well, feel a million and one things at once. She should let him go. But she didn't want to.

"Don't. I can't do this. I wanted to be chill, but it's not me," he said. "I want you. I don't want to talk or rehash the past. I just want sex and maybe to hold you the rest of the night so I can pretend for a few short hours that things are normal. I know that's not what you want, and I completely appreciate where you are coming from, but I can't turn it off. I never have been able to around you."

God.

This was the one thing she'd never been able to understand about Logan. He played to win but he played from a place of total honesty. Maybe that was why it was so hard to walk away. Even though she knew that if she stayed, she could get hurt, his honesty made her want to try. Try to figure out a way to get what they both wanted.

"I'm not trying to make this harder on you," she said.

"I know," he said. "Let me leave. You can go back to the party and I can do what I do best."

Quinn wondered what he thought he did best, but didn't ask. There had been too much talking and it hadn't moved them any closer to sorting anything out. She moved quickly, straddling him and putting her hands on his shoulders.

She saw the surprise on his face, yet couldn't really read the emotions in those bright blue eyes of his. She didn't need to. "I want this too. I think I was trying to justify it to myself, but the truth is, it's been a long time and I've missed you, Logan."

He put his hands on her waist; she felt his fingers squeeze her. "If this isn't what you want…leave now or let me leave."

She leaned down then, her lips brushing his before

she kissed him long and deep. She pushed her hands into his thick hair and held him underneath her. Pretended for the moment that he was in her control.

His tongue brushed over hers and she shifted on his lap, taking the kiss deeper. She had been kidding herself when she'd thought that she wasn't going to have sex with him on the beach.

This was Logan. The one man who still haunted her. The guy she'd never been able to really stop judging every other man by. And she needed this. She needed to have sex with him as an adult so she could stop idealizing that college relationship.

She was sure that sex with him would be as mediocre as it had been with all the other guys she'd dated in the last few years. That something had changed in her and there was no going back to those wild years. But she quickly realized how wrong she was as Logan's hands slipped down the backs of her thighs and he raised himself up, his abdomen tightening underneath her. She wrapped her legs around him and he paused, resting his forehead against hers.

Quinn opened her eyes, stared into his, then closed them again. It was too intense. She felt him all around her, his exhalations brushed over her face as his chest bumped her breasts.

She opened her eyes again and this time he was watching her. "I know what you said, but are you sure?"

That old hurt that had lingered for so long inside her soul started to melt a little bit. He'd given her more chances to walk away than any other man would. "I'm where I want to be tonight."

"I'm so glad," he said as he tugged her T-shirt up in the back.

She felt the cool summer breeze on her skin a moment before his warm palm was on the small of her back, just holding her with that one touch as he shifted underneath her. "Are you on the pill? I know that question seems awkward, but I'd rather know now than find out you aren't at the wrong moment."

She nodded. "Me too. Yes, I am. Also, I'm healthy, so nothing to worry about on that front."

"Me too. Just had my yearly physical for the board so I can keep my job as CEO," he said.

"Glad to hear it," she said, putting one hand on his shoulder. He looked into her eyes again and something changed inside her. She knew she'd told herself this was to close the door on the past and finally move on from him, but there was something about this that felt new and different. And if she were being honest with herself, it had absolutely nothing to do with the past.

Quinn shoved the thought aside as she felt his hand in her hair, cupping the back of her head as he kissed her again. It was slow and seductive. Not the starter gun at the beginning of the race, but more of a tentative testing of the waters.

# Four

The Jack Daniel's hadn't really made a dent in his temper or caused him to forget anything, but the touch of Quinn's lips was doing just that. He shoved everything aside but the fiery redhead in his arms and focused on her as if she were a million-dollar deal he didn't want to lose.

Her lips were full against his; her hair was soft and smelled like spring when the blossoms in his mother's orangery bloomed. He held her gently though what he really wanted was to roll her beneath him and let go of all his inhibitions. But he knew that would be too much.

No matter that they had always gone full-on

when they competed, Logan had always been smart enough to keep the darkest part of himself from her. His intensity when he was trying to be normal was off the charts, so there was no way going all-out wouldn't overwhelm her.

She sucked his lower lip into her mouth and bit him lightly. He ran one hand down her back, cupping her thigh as he thrust his hips toward hers. Her skin was soft and smooth, her legs bare. He ran his finger up underneath the hem of her shorts, caressing the back of her legs as she drove him out of his ever-loving mind sucking on his lip.

Finally he tore away from the kiss and rested his forehead against hers. She put her hands on his cheeks and ran her thumb along his jaw, causing him to grapple for self-control. He wanted this night with Quinn to last forever so he needed to be more than a five-minute man with her right now. Because he wasn't fooling himself that he'd get more than this one night with her.

In the light of day, given his current fucked-up life situation, this was all the two of them could have. And it was so good that he wanted to binge on all of Quinn. Just give in to the fire that was burning between the two of them. But he liked the slow burn.

"What are you doing?" she asked, rubbing her finger over his bottom lip and making his dick even harder.

He was getting harder and harder and, for the life

of him, it wasn't easy to remember why he was trying to go slow. This was Quinn, for fuck's sake. She'd always rendered his control nonexistent.

"Trying to make this last. But damn, woman, I forgot how fast you get to me," he said. His words were meant to be calming—for himself. But his voice was low, guttural with need, and he stopped trying to hold back. Stopped pretending he could be anything other than his most basic self.

"I didn't," she said, pushing her hands between their bodies and undoing the buttons of his shirt, parting it to drop a kiss in the middle of his chest next to the chain holding the gold coin medallion his father had given him when he'd become CEO. "You make me hotter and wetter than any other guy ever has. I was sort of hoping time would have dulled this, but…"

*No such luck*, he thought.

He reached for the hem of her dress and lifted it over her head. She shivered as the night breeze brushed over her skin and he wrapped his arms around her, drawing her against his chest to warm her up. Her hard nipples pushed into his chest and the lace of her bra was soft against his skin. She wrapped her arms around his neck and twined her fingers together there.

Their eyes met and, for a moment, he forgot everything but Quinn. She shifted again and his erection hardened as she rubbed herself against him. He groaned and sprawled one hand wide against the small of her back, holding her, guiding her as she rocked against him, trying to get her to rub herself against the tip of him. When she did, his head dropped back and he said her name softly like a refrain in time with the movements of her hips.

She laughed softly and he felt her mouth against the column of his neck as she sucked and kissed her way down his body. She shifted, the exquisite movements of her hips stopping as she did so. But he felt her fingers, long and cold, grazing over his stomach and down the center of his body.

He flicked the catch of her bra open with two fingers and then pulled it down her arms. She lifted one and then the other to allow him to remove it. She started to reach for the fastening on his shorts, but he stopped her.

He put his hands on her waist and shifted back so he could see her. In the dark of night, with only the moon and stars, he couldn't see her skin clearly but knew she had freckles all over her body and that her nipples were a brownish pink color. He flicked his fingers over her nipples and felt them tighten under his touch.

He drew one finger down the center of her body as she'd done to him, circling her belly button, flicking the tiny gold hoop that she had there. From memory, he knew that playing with her piercing turned her on. She shifted her hips against his thighs, parting her legs as she did so. He continued to tease her belly button, needing her to be as ready as he was.

Every touch of her hands drove him closer and closer to the edge, and they both weren't even naked yet.

She pulled his head to hers and, as their lips met, part of him wondered if this was nothing more than a fevered summer dream. This woman he'd wanted for too long but hadn't realized until this moment.

One thing about Logan was that he wasn't just driven in business; his passion applied to every aspect of his life. He made love to her with the same intensity that he negotiated a deal in the boardroom. No part of her body was overlooked, no detail was too small to escape his attention. And, surprisingly, he seemed to remember everything that had turned her on all those years ago.

She pushed his shirt off his shoulders, which made him stop fondling her belly button piercing. But her body was still throbbing and even though he'd said he wanted to take it slow, she was ready to have him inside her. She wanted to forget everything except this man and make this night one she'd always remember.

Quinn reached for the button on his shorts but he stopped her again; this time she pushed his hands away. She got that he wanted the slow tease but she wanted him *now*. She undid the button and then lowered his zipper, reaching into the opening to take him in her hand and stroke him. He groaned her name, a guttural sound that seemed to be drawn from inside the depths of him.

"Oh, I'm not going to last, Ace," he said. "And I have it on good authority women like it to be longer than thirty seconds."

She couldn't help the laugh he drew from her. "That's true, but I want to touch you. I want you naked on the blanket so I can enjoy every second of you."

"You have to be naked too. Equality and all that," he said.

"Fine with me," she said, standing and stepping out of her underwear. She was momentarily glad it was night because she hadn't had a bikini wax recently. But then Logan's hands were on her legs, caressing his way up the length of them as he stood next to her. He cupped her naked butt and drew her forward, rubbing his erection against her center, and she had the feeling he didn't really care if she'd had a bikini wax or not.

She pushed his shorts down with his underwear and the tip of his erection bumped her stomach as he stepped out of his shorts. He put one hand between her shoulders and kept the other on her butt, tugging her to him. His mouth came down on hers hard, his tongue pushing into her mouth and his cock rubbing against her mound. She held on to his shoulders and realized he hadn't been joking when he'd said he might not last.

He'd gone from smooth, sophisticated lover to a man with an unquenchable need, and she loved it. This was what she wanted from him. Not the playing at being a gentleman when she knew that underneath his civilized exterior beat the heart of a warrior. A man who was fighting to take everything the world had—and tonight, everything that she had— to give him.

She met his passion with her own. No longer having to temper herself because he wasn't tempering himself. She grabbed his shaft, stroking his length, reaching lower to cup him. She squeezed gently before she tore her mouth from his and kissed her way down his chest. Biting at his pec, which flexed as she did so. He made that groan that sounded like her name again. His hands were in her hair as she moved lower on his body. She kept stroking him with her hand as her mouth drew nearer and she licked the tip of his erection, sucking him into her mouth as his hands tightened in her hair. He reached for her breasts, cupping them in his hands as she sucked him deeper into her mouth. He flicked his fingers over her nipples, and she felt the warmth between her legs.

Quinn was so hot for him, needed him now, but didn't want to stop sucking him. He pulled his hips back and lifted her into his arms, falling to his knees while cushioning the landing for her. They were facing each other again and he framed her face with his hands. In the moonlight, she couldn't see the expression in his eyes but had no doubt of what he wanted next. He pulled her down next to him on the blanket.

She reached for his body, not done with caressing him, but he caught her hand and drew it up above her head. He captured her other hand and held both wrists lightly in his grasp. He knelt next to her torso, his big body crouched and ready, his cock shooting out toward her, his breaths sawing in and out as he looked at her. He drew his free hand down the center of her, starting at her forehead. She sucked his finger into her mouth when he brushed it over her lips and then felt the wetness as he continued his path along her chest.

He ran his damp finger around each of her nipples before moving lower, flicking her piercing before he placed his palm over her mound. He pushed down with the heel of his palm, rubbing his hand over her clit, and then she felt his finger parting her. The air was cool for a moment against her sensitive flesh but then his finger was there. Flicking and rubbing against her. Her hips lifted as she tried to get more but he wouldn't be rushed. He drove her slowly toward the edge of her control. She felt her orgasm, right there just out of her reach, and struggled against his hold on her wrists, trying to touch him. Instead he just brought his mouth to hers as he plunged two fingers into her and drove her over the edge.

* * *

Logan felt a drop of precum on the tip of his cock and knew he was going to spill himself all over Quinn if he didn't get inside her now. But watching her orgasm, driving her to the edge, was the biggest turn-on of all. She was always the one in control. Always the one who kept part of herself back. Except just now. Just now he'd taken it from her and, after a long day when he'd felt like nothing was in his power, he'd needed that.

He leaned over her and kissed her, petting her between her legs until her orgasm subsided. She shifted underneath him, spreading her legs open and tugging her hands free from his grip. He let her go, moving so he was on top of her, shifting his hips until the tip of his erection was at the opening of her body. She was moist and soft and ready for him.

He almost hesitated but she grabbed his ass, pushed her feet into the blanket and drove herself up against him. He thrust deep inside her. She was tight and he hoped he didn't hurt her as he entered her. He kept himself fully seated inside her until he felt her body soften around him and then he pulled back and drove inside again.

She kept one hand on his butt and drew the other up his back. Her fingers softly moved along his spine as her mouth was on his, sucking his tongue deep into her mouth. He rocked against her harder and harder. He felt his own orgasm building and wanted to make it last, wanted her to come again with him, but wasn't sure he had any power to slow down. He reached between their bodies, flicking her clit with his finger, and she sucked harder on his tongue. Her hips moved urgently against his, his own moving like pistons as he tried to get to the edge and then over it. He kept pumping into her even as his orgasm hit. She bit his tongue and then tore her mouth free of his as she called his name out loud. He buried his face in her neck as his orgasm slowly passed, bracing himself on his hands and knees to keep from crushing her with his weight.

Logan felt her hands in his hair, twirling it through her fingers as he slowly came back into himself. He rolled to his side, pulling her with him, and she cuddled close to him. His breathing slowed and so did hers. He knew he should say something, needed to talk to her, but he had no words.

Didn't want to ruin this moment by trying to explain it or justify it. He wanted to just hold her with the summer stars above them and not think for a few damned minutes. And he could. He felt her drop a kiss on his chest and then she shivered as the breeze blew. He reached for his shirt with his free arm, draped it over her, and she smiled up at him.

As their eyes met, he knew that the words he didn't want to say were right there hovering, ready to come out. But he wasn't a man to make fake promises and he knew until everything was out about what he'd done to Williams, Inc., he couldn't ask her to let him back in her life. He couldn't reach out and take her with him because he was in a car that was going too fast and had no brakes. And if this night had proven anything to him, it was that Quinn mattered to him.

She had calmed his monkey mind and given him a chance to breathe. She'd made it okay to forget for just a little while and he wanted…well, something that he didn't dare take because she deserved better.

Hell, she always had.

"Don't," she said.

"What?" he asked. But he knew. That moment he'd had right after they'd come was gone. The world was waiting and there was no denying it.

"Think. Don't think, Logan. Lie here with me for just a little bit longer," she said softly, but even in her voice, he could hear that she knew it was too late.

He laid back because he was stubborn that way. He hated this part of himself. The part that always managed to break things even when he was trying to be careful. He could broker deals and increase profit margins, but when it came to the personal, he had no subtlety. That was glaringly obvious as he heard Quinn sigh and then sit up, reaching for her clothes.

"I need a shower. Want to come back to the house I've rented for the week and clean up?" she asked. "Or are you heading back to the bonfire?"

"I'm with you, Ace, if you'll have me," he said. "I know I—"

She put her fingers over his mouth to stop him from talking. "Let's just get dressed, go to my place, and then we can talk or dissect or whatever it is you think we need to do."

They both got dressed and as she started to walk toward the wooden walkway, he stopped her.

"I wanted to hold you and just forget for a little while longer. I'm just not sure how to do that, Quinn. Please, never think that I wanted this," he said, gesturing to them. "I just don't know how."

"Stop trying to make sure you win, and it will happen."

"This wasn't about winning," he said.

"Are you sure?" she asked.

He wasn't sure. Now that she'd pointed it out, he realized he hadn't wanted to seem like he needed her more than she needed him. And Quinn Murray never needed a man—especially Logan Bisset.

# Five

Adler watched her fiancé getting drunk and acting...well, like the man she'd fallen in love with. He'd
never admit it, but he seemed to be bonding with his
half siblings. The Bissets and his Williams siblings
were taking their cues from him. In the Williams'
family's favor, they'd always known Nick had had a
different dad than Tad Williams. Of course, learning
that it was August had thrown them all.

"He'd going to be so hung over tomorrow," Olivia
said, coming up to her after Iris had left the bonfire.
Quinn had disappeared as well, and Adler had tried
to put on her big-girl panties and socialize as if she
wasn't questioning everything. Looking at the young

woman who was going to be her sister-in-law if this marriage went off, she smiled.

"He definitely is. I have the feeling he won't regret it," Adler said.

"I know I won't," Olivia said. "I recorded him and Zac singing earlier. I'm going to have blackmail material for years."

Adler laughed as she suspected Olivia wanted her to. Nick's youngest sibling and only sister had straight black hair that framed her heart-shaped face. She had dark brown, almost black eyes that were forthright. She was down for a good time, but she was also a very serious woman. She was young—twenty-eight—but everyone knew she was following in Nick's footsteps and would be a serious contender for CEO if he ever stepped aside.

"Are you okay?" Olivia asked as they both took a glass of white wine from the passing waiter.

"Yeah. I mean why wouldn't I be?" Adler really hoped it wasn't obvious how freaked out she was by the news that Nick wasn't who he thought he was. That the media was going to have a field day with the news two titans of industry shared a connection to Nick. It was the kind of juicy scandal the tabloids loved. And she'd always—*always*—hated that kind of media attention.

"We're going to be sisters," Olivia said. "After a lifetime with just guys, I had hoped we could talk and I wouldn't have to front all the time with you."

Adler turned to Olivia and realized what the other woman was saying. She and Olivia had spent some girl-time getting to know each other. She had craved having a close sister bond. She had a few half siblings from her father's numerous affairs, but he had a way with women that made them tend to hate him when he moved on so she'd never had a chance to get close to any of them.

"I do want that," Adler said. "I just don't want to ruin this night for you."

Olivia put her arm around Adler's shoulders. "You can't. We're sisters and I've got your back. So talk to me."

She looked at Olivia for another long minute and then took a deep breath. "I'm freaking out. I mean I wish I could get drunk, like Nick's doing, but I know that won't help, and I have to do some shooting in the morning for the reality TV show—which I'm not sure we should still do. But Quinn is counting on me. And maybe it's better to get ahead of this with some positive media…" She trailed off, realizing she was about to start rambling all of the fears plaguing her.

Olivia shook her head. "I get it. It's easy for Nick to drink because he can't begin to start sorting this out, but that's not you. It's not me either. Want to make a plan? I'm good at this and I'll help however I can. Iris will too. You don't have to worry about anything but your wedding. We can handle the other stuff," Olivia said.

The wedding was one of her chief concerns. Could she marry a man who wasn't who she thought he was? It seemed selfish for her to even be concerned about it, but she had never been the kind of woman who ignored her inner feelings. This was bothering her.

Adler knew the lie hadn't been Nick's, but she also realized this was going to change him in ways she couldn't even begin to guess. She certainly wasn't going to say any of that to Olivia, who watched her as if waiting for something. "You're right. I think it's just so new that I was overwhelmed. I'll make a list and then we can divvy it up."

"Great. Want to do it tonight?"

She started laughing. Olivia was a bit of a bookworm and didn't normally like socializing, so Adler wasn't surprised she wanted to do it now. "No, let's enjoy this party. I think once the word gets out, things aren't going to be like this again."

"You're right. This is the last moment where we know that Nick is both ours and the Bissets. All my life, Dad has told us August Bisset was the boogeyman and I sort of always believed him and thought that his kids, especially Logan, were the same. But now they are related to me…" Olivia let her words fall; she was probably as mixed up about everything as Adler was, albeit from a different perspective. And at that moment, Nick came running over to Adler, scooped her up in his arms and spun her around.

"I love you, Addie. Nothing else matters but you," he said, letting her slide down his body until their lips met and they kissed.

Nothing else mattered. She wanted to believe it as he deepened the kiss and cupped her butt, but she knew no matter how much they both wanted that to be true, the outside world would interfere.

Nick had a way of making that all fade as he pulled her into his arms and danced with her as her father sang about the simple life. She remembered her advice to Olivia and decided to enjoy this moment when everything seemed perfect, because she knew perfection was an illusion.

Juliette Bisset stood on the widow's walk looking out at the horizon. Her husband was in the study with Carlton forming some sort of plan. Tad and Cora Williams had left an hour ago and her mother had retired. She was alone on the walk, wearing the same shawl she'd wrapped Logan in when she'd brought him home from the hospital as a baby. She took a deep breath.

She'd had no idea that Logan was really August's son. She'd just claimed him in her heart as hers. But seeing Bonnie—Cora!—today had thrown her.

On that fateful night when she'd met a young single mother in a small rural hospital, she'd had no idea

who the father of the other woman's baby—babies—
was. But today she knew.

August Bisset. Her own husband.

After all these years, it felt like everything had
been laid to rest. She'd had her dark little secret that
she carried with her until today. Without even a
hint of irony, she had to wonder how she could have
missed that Logan was Auggie's son. They were like
two peas in a pod. Auggie was being overly contrite and saying and doing all the things that…well,
frankly, he'd done over the course of their marriage
every time she'd found out he was cheating.

Juliette had seen in his eyes real sorrow this time.
This was the one thing she hadn't expected to see.
Their marriage had been good since Mari's birth.
They'd slowly made their way into a relationship
where they were both honest with each other, and
that was what hurt the most. Auggie was finally the
man she'd always wanted him to be. The way he'd
been treating her since the revelation that Nick was
his son was evidence of that.

Yet she knew it wouldn't last.

It couldn't.

There was no way, once he realized that she'd lied
about Logan all these years, that he could forgive
her. The baby she'd carried had been stillborn and
she'd made a deal with the single mother who had
expected one child and not twins. A deal to help save
her rocky marriage. But looking back was probably

going to not only ruin her marriage but also break her family. How could she have been so blind?

She was racked with guilt. Over the secret that had seemed so innocent until this afternoon when Cora Williams had shown up and revealed herself to be one and the same as Bonnie Smith. The woman who'd worked for Bisset Industries all those years ago, who'd had an affair with August. And with whom Juliette shared a secret that could be her undoing.

Frankly, Juliette had never paid any attention to August's business since she had carved her own life with her charity work. But now Juliette wished she had. Heck, she'd even avoided meeting Adler's future in-laws because…well, she hadn't wanted any part of August's sharklike behavior to spoil things for Adler. But now she wished— Heck there was a long list of things she wished she'd done.

And they didn't start with meeting Nick's mom. They started back in that hospital room in 1983. The place where she'd first met Bonnie. They'd both just gone through labor, and each was facing the hardest challenge of her life. The deal…it had seemed a simple solution at the time. Juliette would help out the destitute single woman who'd just given birth to twin boys by funding her education and giving her a lump sum of money to set herself up in exchange for one of the twins becoming hers. Replacing the stillborn baby that she'd brought back here to Nantucket and buried in that unmarked grave in the family plot.

She'd loved Logan from the second she'd held him. Had never thought of him as anyone else's son but hers. And bringing the new baby home, the child everyone believed was hers and August's, had given her and August a new start until his eye had wandered again.

Someone cleared his throat and she glanced toward the open sliding-glass door to see August standing there with a tray that had two snifters on it. He stood tall almost six feet, five inches, but he'd lost a bit of that height in the last few years. His once jet-black hair was shot with gray, which only made him seem more distinguished. His jaw was still as strong. His nose a sharp blade that gave him an intense look.

"May I join you?" he asked. His voice was deep, and she closed her eyes as she felt tears burning at the backs of them.

"Baby, I'm sorry. Please let me try to make this right," he said.

She opened her eyes and realized that he'd moved onto the platform and was now crouching in front of her chair. She put her hand on his shoulder. She wanted to let him make it right, but she was torn. Should she just make her confession now? Would it come out? She was pretty sure that Bonnie aka Cora wasn't going to spill it, but if this afternoon had proven anything, it was that secrets had a way of coming out of the shadows.

"It's okay," she said, touching his cheek and feeling the stubble underneath her palm.

He turned his head and kissed her before standing and taking the chair next to hers. "It's not okay. I'm sorry I didn't know about Nick or even that Bonnie had been pregnant. What kind of man was I?"

She reached out for one of the snifters. "A selfish asshole."

"Agreed. I hate that I hurt you twice with this same indiscretion. You know I've changed."

"I do know," she admitted. "It's not for me to forgive. As you said, this indiscretion is something we covered a long time ago. The kids are going to struggle. Especially Logan, as he hates the Williamses as much as you do."

Auggie took a sip of his brandy, rubbing the back of his neck with his free hand. And as she looked at him, she saw what she'd missed earlier: the strain around his eyes. He was taking this hard. Harder than she'd seen him take any news they'd ever received.

"Are you okay?"

He shook his head. "I have a son I didn't know about. I've been in meeting rooms with him over the years and never recognized him…how could I not have?"

Juliette reached over and took his hand in hers,

squeezing it. "You weren't looking for a son. You were looking at a rival, so that's what you saw."

He lifted her hand to his mouth, his lips brushing her knuckles. "I really did hit the jackpot when I met you, Jules. I know I haven't always acted like it, but you are the greatest treasure of my life."

She couldn't stop the tears that fell when he said that. He put his snifter down and lifted her onto his lap, holding her and apologizing. But she knew the tears weren't for what he'd done but for what *she'd* done and the impact it was going to have on her family and this man she loved.

Quinn's rented house was two streets over from his gran's place. As they walked, Logan held her hand and they both took sips from the bottle of Jack. Most of the homes were dark but he could hear the sounds of music and laughter from the backyards. It was a quiet kind of night in this tranquil setting.

Usually being on Nantucket made his skin feel too tight. He wasn't a downtime guy and this trip wasn't really any different. Quinn didn't say much as they walked and she'd kept his shirt on over her dress. He wanted to say something that would make this seem like it was something more than a hookup. His mom always said to be honest and shoot straight.

"What are you thinking?" Quinn asked. "You keep looking over at me as if you want to say something."

"I do. But I'm not sure how to say it," he admitted. As with all deep truths, it was hard to actually voice.

"Then just say it."

He smiled. "My mom would say the same thing."

"Your mom has given you advice on women?"

"Inadvertently. You know today wasn't the first time we've had to confront my dad's infidelities. One time when I was about ten, I thought they were going to break up for good. She was so pissed. She cries when she's mad. She was in the garden dead-heading plants and Dare and Leo and I went out to help. She turned to the three of us, with those wilted flowers in her gloved hand and tears in her eyes, and said, 'Don't lie. Never lie to a woman you love because that just makes the truth hurt that much more.' I didn't have a clue what she was talking about."

"So what are you trying not to lie to me about?" Quinn asked, cutting to the point in that blunt way of hers. Had the magic of the evening faded for her? He was still drifting in the summer evening in a haze of whiskey and regret that he'd ruined their cuddle on the beach.

"Nothing. I don't want to lie about anything. I think we both know that hooking up wasn't what either of us planned, but it feels like more than a hookup to me," he said. Damn, why was he talking so much? He should stop drinking. He saw a trash can near the sidewalk and walked over to throw away the bottle.

"It wasn't what I planned," she admitted. "But I don't regret it or I wouldn't have asked you back here. I know you're not in a good place, Logan. I'd have to be an idiot to read this any other way than we were hot for each other and you needed a distraction."

A distraction.

"No. I mean yes, but you are not just a distraction," he said, rubbing the back of his neck as if that would make things clearer.

She opened the door to the cottage she'd rented and they stepped inside.

He leaned back against the door as he closed it. "I wish we'd done this a few weeks ago. Before…" He stopped himself. Before what? Before he'd set about undercutting his rival who also happened to be marrying into his extended family? No. What he'd meant was before he'd become this guy. The man he was today, who never let anyone get the better of him. He wished…stuff hadn't happened. That somehow he'd have been different in college so that the two of them would have— No, that wasn't it either. He wouldn't change the man he was for anything. He knew that.

"Hey," Quinn said. She stood on the natural woven runner just watching him. "Let's just not lie when it comes up. I want to spend the night with you because I know this is it. You and me are never doing this again, so I want to get every second with you until the sun comes up. What do you want?"

He stared at her. Wondered how he'd ever been

lucky enough to call her his, and knew that he wanted that exact same thing. She was the oasis in the crazy that was his family and this wedding of the year.

"The same. And maybe a shower. I have sand in places that it isn't meant to be."

She threw her head back and started laughing. "Me too. This place has a large master bathroom with a two-headed shower stall and a huge garden tub. Want to join me?"

He followed her down the hall to the master bath and stood there enjoying the sight of Quinn stripping and singing to Taylor Swift's "Lover" as she did so. He had his buzz from drinking but he was certain it came more from being with Quinn than from the alcohol.

He stripped off his clothes and followed her into the shower. He took his time soaping her body, running his hands over her freckled skin and making sure he didn't miss an inch. In the morning, when he had to walk away, he wanted this night to have been enough to last for the rest of his life. Because as Quinn had said, this was it. They weren't going to fall into each other's arms again.

She was a distraction, and he knew she wouldn't approve of what he'd done to Nick's business deal before he'd learned they were half brothers. She wouldn't approve of him at all, he thought. Behavior like that was why they were no longer a couple.

But for this one night none of that mattered.

# Six

Logan was still hung over from last night. He looked around Gran's den at his family and realized the rest of them were in misery, too. His mother was…well, not herself. His father sat in the corner, nursing one of the Bloody Marys that Gran's butler, Michael, had made for them. Zac had a tortured look on his face. Right before coming here, he'd had a confrontation with Iris, his date for the wedding, and was in real hot water.

It turned out that a private conversation Zac'd had in the lobby of his hotel, in which he'd confessed that Iris had paid to date him, had been recorded and the video had gone viral. Iris was angry at Zac, and Logan didn't blame her. But it was just another piece of kindling thrown on the fire that was slowly burning down the Bisset name.

The only silver lining—or silver-plated lining—was that Zac's problem was a welcome distraction from thinking about the situation with Nick Williams—and about Quinn. But his brother was broken. His feelings for Iris had intensified over the course of the weekend, and now his chances with her were virtually nil. Normally, Zac was carefree, looking at the horizon and longing to get back on his yacht and sail away. But even the ocean seemed to be closed to him now. He sat in the den at Gran's house where Carlton looked like he was going to implode if another one of them revealed something scandalous.

"Is this it? Are we all here?" Carlton asked.

Mari breezed into the room alone. Her fiancé, Formula One driver Inigo Velasquez, was racing this weekend. She pushed her Wayfarers up on her head and surveyed them all. "Who died?"

God, Logan loved his little sister.

"Um, Zac was caught on tape saying Iris paid him to be her date. There's been some fallout from that," he said. "I think what you are seeing is that shell-shocked look that comes from being hammered by hurricane-force waves."

"Geez, Zac, are you kidding me?" Mari asked, going over to Michael and taking one of the drinks he'd prepared. "Can I have something to eat, please, Michael? I'm starving."

"Yes, Miss Mari. Anyone else?"

"I'm hungry too," Zac said.

They all joined in asking for food and Michael left to prepare something. It had been a long time since the family had been together in one room. The family he'd grown up a part of and thought he'd known so well until yesterday's revelations.

"What are we going to do?"

"Zac, you have to apologize to Iris. To be honest, this is probably going to be a nice distraction for the paparazzi from the entire Nick thing. But she's not going to see it that way," his mom said. "Then we need to be prepared to present a unified front on…Nick."

"I agree," Carlton said. "I have a statement ready to release and I think that will help to mitigate most of the speculation. I want to stress that Cora Williams kept the name of Nick's father to herself. And it was only when they were forced into the same room that she admitted the truth. We need to continue to stress that there was no ulterior motive in keeping the secret, just two lives that went on separate paths."

Logan wanted to believe things would be that easy, that one statement would make the paparazzi go away. But he knew it wouldn't. As soon as his business deal hit the papers—and it would on Monday—there would be more interest.

"Great. What about business? Are we going to mention that Nick is the CEO of our biggest rival?" Logan asked.

"And that Logan and he hate each other?" Leo asked. "I mean I think most people know that."

"You're not helping, Leo," Dare said. As a politician, he was usually the one to find the most diplomatic way of saying things. Logan realized that he needed his big brother's advice before the news broke on Monday.

"I'm just saying the kind of stuff that's going to crop up on social media. The kind of comments we are going to have to address," Leo pointed out. "Carlton, you know your stuff when it comes to the legitimate press but influencers are going to come for Iris and for Logan once the news breaks. I think my PR team could help Iris with that since I work with influencers all the time."

"I like that idea," Zac said. "Iris isn't talking to me so, can I reach out to her and tell her?"

"Sure," Leo said. "Dad? Should I call my PR team up here?"

His dad looked at Carlton, who nodded. "Do we have time to wait or should we video conference?"

His father put down his drink and stood, and Logan realized the old man was taking control of the situation.

"All of us in this room have a vested interest in making sure that the spin goes our way. Zac, your comment and your decision were unfortunate. We will help you fix it because that's what this family does. Leo and Carlton will work on the message. Everyone needs to smile and stay on message. Adler is your mother's only niece—her last connection to her sister—we are not going to allow anything to ruin her wedding."

His mom rose and walked to his father's side. She seemed motivated now and, while her smile wasn't as bright as it usually was, she was making the effort. "I will make sure that Adler is protected from this as much as I can. Her wedding needs to be her focus."

"Perfect," his dad said. "Logan, reach out to Nick and try to see if you can partner for the golf scramble together. Carlton will try to get some publicity photos of the two of you so we can allay the fears of both boards that this news is going to shake things up."

"How will that help?" Logan asked. "We're still going to be rivals with Williams, Inc."

"We want to look friendly," August said.

"I don't think that's the right message," Logan said.

"I just told you it was," his father shot back.

Logan clenched his jaw. "You're not the CEO anymore, Dad. We need to talk about this."

"Good idea," Mom said. "You two can have a chat on Monday. For now, let's focus on fixing Zac's mess and the wedding."

Iris was a mess and Adler was only a little better. Both of them were struggling to deal with fallout from dealing with the Bissets.

Quinn kept it to herself that she'd slept with

Logan last night. But seeing her friends and how being connected to the Bissets had this kind of impact sharpened her desire to ensure that last night was a one-off.

They were in a private suite at the hotel and her production team had set up to film the manicures and pedicures the bridal party were having this morning. It was just for cutaways later. "Are you doing the golf scramble this morning?"

"Yes," Adler said. "Nick and I want to keep to the schedule. I mean I think that's what we want. He was sleeping when I left, but I asked Olivia to make sure he was at the golf club at eleven. I'm worried about everything falling apart."

"Me too," Iris said. "I'm so sorry, Adler, that everything with Zac has been leaked."

Adler hugged Iris, and Quinn sat there watching the two of them. Just a day earlier she would have said her friends had it all. Men they loved and relationships that were solid. If anything, it just demonstrated that there was no such thing as a perfect one. She'd always known that. Had seen her parents' example: two people who married in a white hot fit of passion and were like fire and water. But she'd thought if she were smarter—like Iris and Adler— she'd be able to find a man who could be a partner to her.

Though, of course, falling into Logan's arms wasn't part of that plan.

"I'm sorry for you," Adler said. "But honestly, I think it will help distract from the scandal of Nick being a Bisset. It's so crazy right now. He's pretending it's not a big deal but he grew up hating August. When he first found out that he was my uncle, I thought it would be a deal breaker for us. Now it turns out August is his father."

"Me too," Iris admitted. "To be fair I know the Williams family way better than the Bissets, but from what I've observed, they aren't that different."

Iris had been friends with Nick in college and had been responsible for introducing him to Adler, who had been her roommate.

"In what way?" Quinn asked. "Logan is so driven, and my impression has always been that his family all have to be number one."

"It's the same with Nick's family. I mean Tad is nicer about it. More of a 'rising tide raises all ships' but he definitely wants them all to rise, if you know what I mean," Iris said. "Also, Tad has always hated August but no one knows why...do you, Adler?"

"No. I mean Nick said that he thought his dad and August had a falling out long before he was born. Interesting that Tad didn't know Cora had an affair with August or that she'd worked for Bisset Industries," Adler said.

"Yeah. I would hate to be her right now," Iris said. "I feel bad about it. But how did she think it would go when Nick met August?"

Adler shook her head and shrugged. "To be honest, I think she thought August wouldn't come to the wedding because he and I aren't close and he hates the Williams family as much as they hate him. He only decided last minute. I'm pretty sure she intended to never be in the same room with him if she could help it."

"I don't blame her," Quinn said. Her phone started pinging. Most of it was from her network wanting to discuss the scandalous rumors coming out of Nantucket. "Adler, who is releasing a statement about Nick?"

"I think it's going to be a joint one later, but I don't have the details. Why?" Adler asked as she glanced down at her painted toenails.

"The network wants deets and I'm stalling, but I am going to have to give them something," Quinn said.

"Let me text Nick and see what he knows," Adler said. She grabbed her phone and Quinn glanced at Iris, who was sitting so stiff and still, as if by keeping her posture perfect, she could hold herself together.

"Iris, you okay?"

"Yes, of course," she said. "I'll weather this. My parents are coming out today to be with me for the rest of the weekend. Mom said keep my head high. Leta told me not to respond to any of the gossip and just pretend that I didn't hear it."

"Does she think that will work?"

"No, but she said it will piss off the gossip sites who want more dirt. Zac is so apologetic, I think he'd say anything to make up for this, but it's too late. Mari said she would stand by me, which means a lot, but some of the other influencers that I've been working with have dropped me."

Iris was a popular influencer who had started a blog in college and transitioned it to a chronicle of being a single-girl-in-the-city as she'd left, growing her audience and her influence. She had hired Zac to pose as her boyfriend because her fiancé had dumped her before the wedding and she had a collab with a couples brand for the weekend.

Quinn got up to hug her friend. This was the reality of the 24/7 lifestyle they were all living. For herself, Quinn knew she was outside the spotlight but still close enough that she was on the radar for some of the paparazzi because they knew she had friendships with Iris and Adler. This weekend was going to shine the spotlight on everyone and the only way she would survive it was to be strong for her friends and to stay away from Logan.

He was in the middle of the spectacle, which he hated. But she knew he'd manage, and it didn't matter if he hated it or not, because he wasn't her man. He was a guy she'd hooked up with for old times' sake. That was all.

Really.

And she wasn't going to let it be more than that.

She couldn't. Because if she did, she might end up like her best friends. And really who wanted to feel like that?

Logan waited until Nick was paired up with one of his groomsmen before he walked into the clubhouse to be paired for the golf scramble. His mother stood to one side, looking elegant and smiling like her world wasn't falling apart.

"Mom, do you have a partner yet?"

"No, honey, I don't. What about you?" she asked.

He'd been planning to find Quinn and pair up with her, but she was busy with her film crew. He had a new respect for Quinn and the job she did. She'd been running around since they'd all gotten here and one of her crew had let it slip that she'd been working since seven this morning. Given how he'd felt when he'd woken up and slipped out of her rented house this morning, he really admired that.

"I don't. Want to join me and we can kick some butt?" he asked her.

"Whose butt?" Leo asked, coming over to stand next to them. "I don't have a partner yet. Are we making it interesting?"

"I'm game," Logan said. "Let's play for bragging rights and, let's say, ten voting shares in the company."

"Boys," Mom cautioned.

"I like it," Leo said.

"I don't. Never wager the company," Mom said. "Pick something else."

"Okay. Once Leo gets his partner, we'll decide. You know Mom and I won the Bridgehampton Scramble for the last three years."

"I do," Leo said. "But I suspect that's because I wasn't competing. And Mom has been carrying you for a while."

"Boys," Mom said, putting her arms around them both and hugging them, "it's because we are Bissets that we win."

"Exactly," Leo said. "Let me go get partnered up and then we can make a wager."

Leo walked away and Logan turned to his mom. She was smiling after his younger brother. "Leo's such a suck-up."

"Because he said I was carrying you?" she asked. "He knows it's not true. He just thinks it's funny. Your dad likes to needle you the same way."

"He does. Has it ever occurred to you that Dare and I are the most like you?" Logan asked.

Her smile dipped for a moment and then she nodded. "You are both a lot like your father too."

"Yeah, but you have a subtlety that he lacks and that I think I inherited."

"You and Leo are determined to make me blush today," she said.

"We just want you to know how much we love you," Logan said.

"Oh, boyo," she said, using her childhood nick-name for him and hugging him close. "I love you so very much too."

Logan hugged her back, holding her longer than he needed to because he sensed that this latest thing with his dad was hurting her more than she let on. He knew how he'd feel if he and Quinn were a cou-ple and some dude showed up saying she was his. And that wasn't even half of what his mom was deal-ing with.

And he wasn't a couple with Quinn, he reminded himself firmly.

He heard Leo cursing and stepped away from his mom to see what had his brother upset.

Juliette shook her head. "He's making a scene."

"I think you should have spanked him more when he was little. He's a bit of a brat."

His mom playfully punched Logan in the arm. "You all are. Let's go see what the problem is."

He followed her over to the table where the part-ner assignments were being managed.

"What's the problem, little Leo?" Logan asked.

"Nothing. There's no problem. Just found out I've been paired with Danni Eldridge."

"Why is her name familiar?" Juliette asked.

"She's a small business owner whose company is being compared to Leo's," Logan said with a smile. "Oh, I think we should make a healthy wager."

"She's not my competition. She's a startup working out of her garage. I have a large warehouse and factory where I produce hand-made quality products."

"So there isn't a problem, right?" Logan asked. His brother's defensive tone belied the notion that her little startup didn't bother him. Leo had started the same way. Hand-making products in his home and growing his business. "Where is she?"

"I don't know," Leo said. "I've never met her and don't know what she looks like."

"Surely you looked her up online," Logan said.

"I did. Her profile picture is a Singer sewing machine," Leo said.

"I'll go and find her," their mom said, moving toward the crowd of wedding guests congregated by the golf carts.

"I think we should wager shares," Logan said.

"Forget it. I don't know her at all. I thought I'd get Dare, but he's paired with some girl I've never met either."

"This just isn't your day, Leo," Logan said.

Before Leo could answer, their mom started back toward them, her arm looped through another woman's. The stranger had dark brown, curly hair and a heart-shaped face. Her eyes were brown and her gaze direct as she got closer to them.

Logan noticed that Leo was staring at her the way Logan was pretty sure he'd been looking at Quinn last night. "Maybe the competition isn't as bad as you thought," Logan said.

"Maybe," Leo said, walking over to the woman and holding out his hand. "Are you Danni? I'm Leo. Leo Bisset," he said. "I've been wanting to meet you for a while now."

"I bet you have," Danni said. "That's why you told the press that you thought my startup was just me trying to hang on to your coattails as you forge a new path."

"Damn," Logan said.

His mom elbowed him in the ribs. "Let's leave the two of them to talk. Leo, we'll meet you at the golf carts."

Logan followed her to the line, trying not to smile too much. There were a lot of times that Leo reminded him of himself. They both had a way of opening their mouths and making things a million times harder. No matter how much he thought he'd changed, there was a part of him that knew if he tried to get serious with Quinn he'd probably put his foot in it with her too.

# Seven

The Nantucket Golf Club was busy with the wedding party and guests all playing eighteen holes. Nick and Adler had hired staff to be at each of the holes with beverages and snacks, and there were photo booths at the odd-numbered holes. Quinn had her camera crew set up on the most picturesque hole to capture everyone who played through. She had been filming some confessional video that she was going to edit as a gift to the couple, so had used her own personal camera.

So far, she thought it was going to be a nice video package to go along with the live wedding coverage. The day was sunny and perfect for June. Quinn wasn't a sentimental person but if she were, she'd think that Mother Nature was giving Adler a nice day to make up for everything that had happened the day before.

Adler was all smiles when she showed up at the hole partnered with her dad, along with Nick and his sister, Olivia, who were also partnered. Toby Osborn was the first one to the tee and Nick was offering his soon-to-be father-in-law some tips while Olivia stood off to the side snapping pictures with her SLR camera.

"How's it going?" Quinn asked Adler.

"Not too bad. I think things are dying down. Carlton has a statement he's going to release to the press this afternoon. Do you want me to have him send it to you too so you can incorporate it into the wedding broadcast?" Adler asked.

Quinn realized that though Adler was smiling, she seemed fragile, like she was barely holding it all together. Quinn hugged her and Adler shook her head and put her hand up.

"Don't. You'll make me cry, and Nick and Dad will both want to know why… Like, honestly, if I have to tell them, will they even get it?"

"Sorry. Yes, have Carlton send it to me. Also, what do you think about you and Nick offering a personal little taped segment that deals with it? Just a quick it-was-a-surprise-but-whatever type thing?" Quinn asked. She was walking a delicate balance here because Adler was one of her best friends. Yet, as a producer, she'd be foolish if she didn't try to get them to talk about the issue on camera. It was the kind of thing that would make viewers who were hungry for gossip tune in, and could be a ratings boon.

"Sure. Can we do it before the rehearsal dinner? We'll both be dressed. Let me check with Nick on the timing," Adler said, going to talk to Nick.

Quinn noticed that Toby had finished taking his shot and waved him over. "I'm making a little video gift for Adler and Nick. Would you mind giving me a message in the booth over there? Just whatever you want to say to them," Quinn said.

"Love to, Q. But my girl looks like she's about to shatter. Is she okay?" Toby asked.

"She's as okay as she can be. I don't know what to do to help," Quinn confessed.

"Me neither. My gut is to do something scandalous to take the spotlight off Nick but…I'm finally with a woman who I think is the one. Is that selfish?" Toby asked.

Quinn shook her head. Toby had left a trail of lovers and scandals behind him and while Quinn knew she couldn't really speak for Adler, she was pretty sure her friend wanted her dad to have the happiness he'd found with Sonia, his latest girlfriend. "She'll be ticked at you if you do. She likes Sonia."

"All right. I'll just stay in a holding pattern for now. Where do you want me to do the taping?"

"That little area over there with the camera." Quinn gestured at the booth. "My PA, Tillie, will take you over."

As Tillie escorted him to the area, Adler came back over to Quinn. "Nick said if we could do the filming around four forty-five that would work with his schedule. He has to do something with his family at four fifteen. We're going to be on a tight clock."

"It will work," Quinn said. "Go tee off."

Adler went back to take her shot and Quinn managed to get Olivia over to the taping area after Toby finished. Nick stood to the side, watching Adler, and she saw a similar...well, *fragility* wasn't the right word for Nick, but he wasn't okay either.

"Hey, Nick, how are you doing today?" she asked.

"Okay," he said.

He reminded her so much of Logan in that moment. There was something about his smile that teased a memory at the back of her mind. The way he was using his natural confidence to mask the fact that there were many things out of his control right now.

"I guess that's the best you can say," Quinn added. She was tempted to mention something about Logan but then stopped herself. She'd had one night with her ex, and that was all it was. She didn't need to try to help Logan become friends with his new half sibling and longtime business enemy.

"Ad told me you want us to discuss the announcement about my real father. What do you have in mind?" Nick asked.

"Whatever you both feel comfortable discussing. I figure we'd look ridiculous if we don't address it. And it will give you both a chance to do it on your terms. Just whatever you want and, if you don't like it, we'll scrap it," she said.

"Really? That doesn't seem like it would be in your best interest."

"It's not, but Adler is one of my closest friends and I approach being a reality TV producer with an absence of malice. I don't want to become success-ful and win the ratings because I hurt either of you and made your lives worse."

"You're one in a million, Quinn. I know Adler values your friendship and I can see why. I hope we can continue to get to know each other and be-come friends."

Spontaneously, she hugged Nick. As the party left the hole, she wondered why Logan hated Nick so much. From everything that Quinn had seen, he was a decent man and one she thought Logan would respect.

Logan couldn't help but chuckle as he watched Leo trying to be chill and failing miserably. It was clear to him that he liked Danni. Their mother was doing her charming thing and keeping the conver-sation moving but his brother was flirting for all he was worth and getting nowhere. As his mom and Danni went to get drinks for the four of them, Logan couldn't resist needling Leo.

"So how's it going with Danni?" he asked as they walked over to the tee to set up their shots.

"I think you know how it's going," Leo said. "And I'm sure it's amusing to you."

"It is," Logan admitted. "After yesterday, it's reassuring to see that some things never change."

"How do you mean?" Leo asked.

"You and women you actually like," Logan said. "You just can't lower your guard and be real."

"Like you're such an expert at that," Leo said.

"I'm not. I suck at it too. As much as we both hate it, we are very similar in a lot of ways."

"I don't hate to admit it," Leo said. "I've always tried to be like you...but better."

Logan shook his head. His youngest brother never gave an inch. Actually, now that he thought about it, Danni Eldridge probably didn't stand a chance once Leo decided he was going after her.

"You try. That's all you can do," Logan said. "I wish Dad had come today. I know he thinks it's better if he stays away, but he loves golf, and it might have been good for him and Mom to be partners."

"You think so? She still looks like she's upset with him," Leo said as he glanced over at her. "I don't blame her. I'm mad at him and it's not even close to being the same."

Logan nodded. "Dad screwed up. I wonder if he thought he was doing the right thing when it happened."

"He didn't know Nick's mom was pregnant," Leo said. "He probably just figured his affair had ended, and Mom was pregnant with you, so he might have been happy to have it be over."

Logan nodded. Was that what his father had felt? It was always so hard to judge. His siblings all thought that he and August were the closest and, to be fair, they were close when it came to leading Bisset Industries. But personally he doubted he knew his father any better than the rest of his siblings. To be honest, his father never revealed much.

Logan thought his father had a certain charm, but he could also be very brusque—even with their mother. How did a woman love someone like that? Could she? He realized he wasn't just thinking about his dad but, really, he wondered if Quinn could find something inside of him—no. He wasn't going to go down that path. It was just that since he'd left her bed, he'd been missing her.

He could say that one night was all he wanted but being surrounded by all these couples, not just Adler and Nick, but the other couples here, had an effect on him. Even seeing Iris and Zac together, who were paired up and not speaking to each other as they played, made Logan long for more with Quinn.

Logan had always prided himself on being an island. On not needing anything but the next win. But for the first time he saw the price that winning had on personal relationships. He didn't say it out loud to Leo, though he was pretty sure his father had thought that he'd won by having his affair, not getting caught, and moving on. He ate up that kind of conquest. Logan tried not to dwell on the fact that he'd been that kind of man too at one time.

Logan hadn't ever cheated on Quinn when they'd been together in college, but there had been times when he'd thought about it. It would have just been a subtle dig at her because she was smart and clever, and part of him had wanted to see if he could fool her. Luckily, he'd been intelligent enough to know that was a losing path.

How had his father not seen that?

Leo left to flirt with Danni again and his mom came over to take her shot. "You're looking so serious, boyo."

"I'm just thinking about Dad and wondering why he does the things he does," Logan admitted. "I mean—"

"Don't worry about it. I wonder the same thing all the time. I think sometimes he does it just to see if he can get away with it. Other times I think…well, he might stumble into something and though he regrets it when it's over, he never can admit he made a mistake."

"What good would admitting it do?" Logan asked. He had a feeling he might be in a situation where everyone was going to hate him in a few days, and he wasn't sure how to handle it. He should probably just come clean but he was embarrassed by his actions. As he always was. He hated that he had to win at any cost and it was only after he crossed the finishing line or put a tick in the win column that he looked back to see how it affected those around him.

This wasn't going to be easy for anyone to hear and at this moment he didn't want to make them all angry with him.

"It lets everyone around you know that you acknowledge you screwed up and that the hurt you caused wasn't your intention. After the affair and before Mari was born, things changed with your dad and I. It was the first time that he realized by using arrogance to brazen his way through it, he was hurting me, and he was hurting you and your brothers. He decided at that moment that we meant more than his pride," she said.

"Did he?"

"I thought so," she said. But in her tone, he could tell that she wasn't so sure anymore.

Logan wanted to find the words to tell her that everything would be okay, but he didn't know that for certain. Their family was being ravaged by something even he couldn't figure a way out of.

The clubhouse was abuzz with guests sharing stories of their triumphs on the golf course. Quinn stayed toward the back of the room, filming with her crew, but as the crowd thinned out, she sent her team to lunch and asked them to meet back at her rented house around three. Though she was working, she was also a guest and wanted a few minutes to enjoy her friend's wedding as a guest. Also she'd noticed Logan making his way toward her and she wasn't sure she wanted her coworkers to see them chatting.

She'd hoped to be over him, but just the few moments she'd seen him today had proven that it would be difficult. That last night hadn't closed anything for her but instead had reopened emotions she'd thought had long ago subsided.

She should have known better.

It had taken her too long to get over Logan.

"Done working for the day?" he asked as he stopped next to her.

"For the moment. The crew is grabbing lunch," she said. "How'd you do?"

"Okay. Beat Leo, which is all that I cared about," Logan said.

She found that hard to believe. There were so many people here that Logan saw as rivals even if she just started with the Williams family. "Really?"

"No, not really, but I'm trying to be gracious. I beat everyone except Nick…we tied," Logan said.

"The two of you are very similar. Probably comes from all those years of battling each other and watching your fathers battle—"

"Yeah, about that," Logan said sardonically. "You're not wrong. Regardless of DNA, Nick is still a Williams through and through, and it's going to take some time before I can see him differently."

She had suspected as much. "Does Williams still mean enemy?"

"Yes," he said then shoved his hand through his hair, ruffling it. He looked almost boyish with the thick blond hair sticking up. "I know it shouldn't. I mean even before we learned about the half sibling thing, he was marrying my cousin. But at the same time, we've been fighting them in the boardroom for as long as I can remember. The first summer Dare and I went to work with Dad, he was setting up a deal that Tad Williams undercut him on and won. It's hard to change years of thinking overnight."

"No one's asking you to," she said.

"I am. I'm asking myself to change, but it's hard, Quinn. Also…"

She waited to see if he was going to continue but he stopped as he watched Adler and Nick standing together. Nick had his arm around her.

"I'm an ass," he said. "I mean, how could I not see how much Adler loves him? I—I have to get out of here. Can you leave?"

She could. But did she want to? Of course, she didn't want to let him go alone when he'd asked to be with her, but at the same time, if she did go… There was no pretending any more that she wasn't starting to care about the man Logan was today. Not the vestiges of what he'd been in college but the man before her, who was so much more complicated.

"Quinn?"

"Yeah, I'll go with you," she said.

They stepped outside and it was almost as if he took a huge breath. "Sorry about that. I did something before I came here that I regret," he said as they walked away from the clubhouse.

"What?"

"A business thing," he said. "It's complicated and probably boring, but Nick is going to be very unhappy, as will most of my family now that he's 'one of us.'"

"What did you do?"

"Just ruined a deal he has spent the last few months putting together," Logan admitted.

"Why would you do that?" she asked. "He's marrying your cousin."

Logan shook his head. "I don't know."

But she knew he did. "You hate to lose, right? Doesn't matter if there is human roadkill on the side of the superhighway that is Logan. You know that Adler is going to be devastated by this. And it's going to put a strain on things with her and Nick days into their—"

"Do you think I don't regret it?" he asked. "I do. You're right. I didn't think it through, and I thought it was sort of a moral victory because him marrying Adler felt like he got one over on us."

"Honestly, you make me crazy. Not everything is a competition," she said. How had she thought that he'd changed?

"Yeah, I know. I realized that when I walked into Gran's house and saw the devastation that my father had caused by being selfish. I thought it was just a friendly rivalry with Nick, but it wasn't. I was just trying to make sure I came out on top, just like you said, regardless of who I hurt to do it."

He turned away, his hands on his hips and his head bowed. "I can't stop it. What I've set in motion can't be changed. But I wish it could. I think until I saw how Dad's actions were hurting us all, I never got the effect my actions could have on my family."

She stood there for a moment, seeing him this way, knowing that he'd shown her this vulnerability because he trusted her. And…well, it drew her to him. She knew Logan wasn't perfect and, as much as it might make her seem like she wasn't smart, she always knew that it was his imperfection that got to her. His flaws made him human and real to her, and that was something she couldn't resist.

She went over to him and hugged him. He hugged her back. They didn't say anything else and, really, what else was there for either of them to say?

# Eight

Logan's quiet moment with Quinn didn't last long. His father texted him to discuss the business ramifications of the upcoming announcement dealing with the scandal of Nick's parentage. He left Quinn to head to his gran's house and found his father sitting not in the study as he usually was but on the sweeping back porch that overlooked the ocean in the distance.

"How was the golf?" his dad asked when he arrived.

"I beat Leo and tied Nick. Mom and this new girl, who is in Leo's field of business, played fair games."

"Your mom didn't play well?" his father asked.

"No, Dad, she didn't. She is doing a good job of

being the perfect hostess, but we both know she's not on her A game."

"I know," his dad said. "I have no idea how to fix this."

"Me neither," Logan said. "Dad, what were you thinking?"

August rubbed the back of his neck, got up from the rocker and moved to the porch railing. "I can't say. When I was younger, the challenge drove me."

It wasn't much of an answer because Logan knew his father still liked a challenge. So did that mean he wouldn't rule out cheating on Juliette again?

"You wanted to talk business?" he asked.

"Yes. Carlton is already working on the spin, but I saw something…an article in a small paper about someone buying the patent to a new energy-efficient, low carbon emissions grain turbine."

"What about it?" Logan asked. His dad couldn't possibly know that he'd been the one to buy it. He'd done it through a small company he'd purchased under an LLC he'd started in college. There was no connection to Bisset Industries.

"Just thought it was curious as that patent had been one that I know Williams, Inc., has been trying to purchase for a long time. Just seemed odd that it would be snapped up from under them," August said.

"It is odd, but you know business is business."

"Until it's family," August said.

His dad knew. Somehow his father seemed to

know it was him. "Yeah, well, things happen. I'd say that Nick didn't get as many of your genes as he should have if he let it slip away."

"You think?" August turned to face him. His appearance was just as intimidating as it had always been. His hair might be salt-and-peppered now and there were more sunlines around his eyes despite the fact that he had skin care treatments to stay younger looking.

"Dad, if you have something to say, just say it," Logan said.

"Confession is good for the soul," August said.

"Is it? Then why did you wait so long to tell us you'd had an affair while Mom was pregnant with me?" Logan asked. The rise of anger inside him was almost unstoppable. He turned away from his father to stop himself from blurting out all the other things he wanted to say. He was pissed. They all were. Their father had always been a strong and domineering force in their family but now... Logan looked at him and saw a man who wasn't who Logan had always believed he was.

"That's none of your business. It was between Mom and me. I'm asking you about a business deal. Did you buy up the patent?"

"Yes."

"Damn it, Logan. He's family now."

"He wasn't when I did it. And he's an ass. Just because he's suddenly my half brother doesn't change all the times he's dicked us over in business. I'm not going to just smile and shake hands. Sorry if the timing of my purchase isn't ideal for whatever you and Carlton have planned."

"Kid, it's not ideal because your cousin is marrying him on Saturday. She's family. This is going to hurt her."

He knew that. He'd wrestled about that very fact for longer than anyone would believe, even his father. But his need to beat Nick had outweighed Adler's possible hurt feelings. "I don't think Adler cares about business."

"Me either, but she does care about our rivalry with his family."

Logan shook his head and almost walked away. "Would you have made a different decision? If the opportunity had come to you instead of me, would you have passed?"

"No," August said. "I wouldn't have. But I always thought you had some of your mom's kinder side."

"I do. I'm definitely more charming than you are," Logan pointed out.

"Yes, but you're just as dangerous as I am," August said. "I think we need to let Nick know before it comes out on Monday."

"He'll be on his honeymoon," Logan said. "It can wait until he gets back. I mean he sort of has enough to deal with at this moment."

August looked at him and Logan stared right

back. No matter what his dad wanted to do with this situation and the new son he'd found, Logan couldn't change a lifetime of animosity overnight. He'd been willing—hell, not willing, but had thought he'd try for Adler's sake—but if he were being honest, he hated that Nick was related to them.

He hated that the man who'd been his rival in business for more than a decade was his half brother. He kept using *half* in his mind to make the relationship seem more distant, but it didn't change the fact.

Nick Williams was now a blood relative.

"It's your decision," August said. "But from a man who's just had a secret explode when he wasn't ready for it, I can tell you, it's better to confront things on your terms instead of trying to manage the fallout."

His dad turned to head back into the house and Logan was going to just let him leave. But Logan reached out and touched his shoulder as he walked past.

"I'm sorry, Dad. I don't know what it is about me, but I just can't stand to lose. And if I see a chance to win, I have to take it."

His father nodded. "It's the Bisset in you. You get that from me."

"The golf scramble was really successful," Quinn said as she met up with Adler and Iris in the afternoon. Adler looked less stressed than she had been earlier. It was as if the bride-to-be had entered some sort of numb zone. The only reason Quinn thought that was from her years of filming destination weddings. Some brides just got tighter and tighter the closer they got to the ceremony and then others, like Adler, chilled out and nothing fazed them.

While Quinn normally preferred the chilled-out bride over a bridezilla, she wasn't sure this was healthy for her friend. "Did anything else happen?"

"When?" Adler asked as one of Iris's glam squad hovered around her doing her hair for the rehearsal dinner.

"At the family meeting?" Quinn asked.

"No. They just finalized the press release. Which is so bizarre. Nick's mom wasn't at the meeting. Nick said she's freaking out. I don't know her that well, so I'm not sure if I should reach out to her or just ignore the entire thing," Adler said. "Olivia's been cool, but she always has been. Carlton wanted everyone to pose for a picture, but Tad Williams refused. I thought it was going to get dicey, but then everyone just sort of moved on."

"I'm sorry you are dealing with this," Iris said.

"It's not your fault. Dad sort of said that it was ironic that I thought I was marrying someone so solid and stable and then this happened. I think he was trying to help," Adler said.

"I'm sure he was. He mentioned to me that he could do something outrageous if I thought it would help you," Quinn said.

"Oh, God, no. I'm not sure I'm ready for that," Adler said.

"I know. I told your dad you were handling it fine and that you liked him happy and…well, father-like," Quinn said.

"I do. I need something to be consistent and steady in all this," Alder said. "I know I shouldn't make this all about me—"

"You're the bride, you're totally allowed to," Iris said.

"Agree," Quinn added. "It is all about you."

"Nick is freaking out. He keeps trying to be all, *I'm cool with it*. But he really hates Uncle Auggie. He was willing to be cordial for this weekend but learning that he's his real dad has him thrown."

Quinn's phone started vibrating like crazy where she'd set it on the table. "I bet."

She wanted to be a good friend and just stay focused on Adler. Like, was that a hard thing to do? Her dad always said it wasn't like she was a brain surgeon; she could have a conversation without looking at her phone. But…

"Just answer your phone," Adler said. "I hope it's not anything urgent."

She smiled at her friend. "I'm sure it's not. I want to be here for you."

"Honestly, Quinn, you being the producer of the wedding show is huge for me. I think I would have bolted last night if it had been anyone else," Adler said. "Go ahead. I'm going to try to text Dad and make sure he knows I'm okay."

Iris was deep in discussion with one of her glam squad, so Quinn picked up the phone and turned her back on Adler.

She glanced at the first text, which was a link to a news story push from one of the wires. Skimming it, she saw it was the news that Nick was August Bisset's biological son. "It's just that press release Carlton sent."

"Good," Adler said. "Any reaction?"

She scanned the newsfeed and realized that it was pretty tame. "No, but it has just gone out. I was waiting to alert my boss. Do you mind if I go and call in? I want to let them know we are on top of the situation."

"'Situation,'" Adler said. "That's what my wedding has become."

Quinn turned around and walked over to her friend, pocketing her phone as she went. "No. It hasn't. Not for you and not for Nick. To the outside world, it might be, but who cares about that. Everyone who matters to you will know—"

"I know that," Adler interrupted. "Dad says a version of that all the time, but the truth is I hate it. I want people to not notice me, not talk about me. But from the moment I was born, everyone has."

Quinn hugged Adler. She didn't know what to say to help her friend. Words weren't going to fix that bit of brokenness deep inside Adler. Words couldn't change how much she hated to see her photo or her name in the press. Words couldn't help, but a hug could. Friendship could.

"I know I'm so blessed and so lucky and I have Nick. He's my rock, but… I just wanted a quiet, simple wedding. I mean I know I agreed to have it televised, but that's because I thought I could control the narrative that way," she said. "I'm not whining… I mean I am a bit. I'm feeling sorry for myself, I guess."

"You're allowed to. Honestly, you're way better than a lot of the brides we film and you've had a lot more thrown at you."

"Thanks for saying that. I'm sorry I sort of lost it a second ago. Go call your boss. I don't want you to get into hot water because of this," Adler said.

"You're welcome. You can lose it as many times as you want. It's all about you, Ad, I mean that. I won't get into hot water. I just like to keep on top of my boss, so she thinks I'm efficient."

"Then go. Do that. I'll be fine. Iris made me glam, I'm going to sit here and enjoy that," she said.

Quinn took her friend at her word and stood. She noticed that Iris looked over at her when she did so, and Quinn nodded at Adler. Iris walked over to sit with the bride-to-be as Quinn walked out to do her job. She was a friend first, but she was also there to work.

Something she kept forgetting, between Adler and Logan.

* * *

Cora Williams hadn't shown up at the meeting at her mother's house and Juliette couldn't decide if that was a good or bad thing. The two of them weren't friends and had nothing in common. Except for that one secret. The one that was getting closer to being revealed the more time they spent together. Now it seemed foolish that she'd never made an effort to meet Adler's soon-to-be mother-in-law.

What would she have done if she had? Somehow tried to convince her niece to break off her engagement? God knew she'd never been a great sister, and Mari would argue that she hadn't always been a good mother, but Juliette had tried. She'd done her best.

But she had a feeling that wasn't enough.

She took a sip of the gin and tonic that Michael had made for her and then sighed. The press release was done, so there was nothing else to worry about, right? Juliette knew differently but for now she was going to have to put on her hostess smile and act like everything was good.

The announcement was just one more little chink in the image of their "perfect marriage" she'd fought so hard to project since Mari's birth. It was like it was okay for her to see the ugly cracks from the inside but she had hated when one of August's affairs was made public. She could only fake smile for so long before she crumbled.

And this time…well, this time was worse. Everyone—especially Auggie—was being so sweet to her. They were treating her as the injured party almost the same way they were acting toward Nick. But she knew that if the truth really came out, no one was going to look at her with sympathy.

Maybe she was borrowing trouble.

"What are you doing out here all alone?"

She turned to see Vivian standing there watching her. Her mom was the strongest woman Juliette knew. She'd buried a husband, a child, and withstood financial ups and downs. Yet she still managed to seem untouchable. Juliette envied her mother that.

"Thinking."

"And drinking?"

"Yes, Mom."

"Should I join you?" she asked, moving closer to her. Her mother always smelled faintly of Chanel No. 5. Her hair was now more gray than blond, but her eyes were forthright and she held herself with the strength of a woman who could handle anything.

"If you want to."

She rang a little bell on a table near the door of the sitting room and a moment later Michael appeared with a martini. He refreshed Juliette's gin and tonic and then left.

"Remember when you came home and told me you were engaged to Auggie?"

Juliette sighed. She'd been so in love with him. He'd been tall, dark and handsome. A forceful man with an easy smile and the kind of charm that made everyone like him. He was top of their class at college and they'd started out as friends and then fallen in love.

"Yes. You weren't sure about him."

"I wasn't. I could tell he was a little too smooth," Vivian said. "But you knew he was the one. I tried to warn you, but you got your back up—rightly so—and I let it be. I've held my tongue when he had affairs and even when they went public."

"I know, Mom," she said. "Is that about to change?"

"I'm not sure. I don't know what I can say to you that you don't already know. Auggie has always had a wandering eye and I guess you should be thankful that it's taken this long for a child of his to show up—"

"Mom!"

Oh, God, were there more? She should have put an end to the philandering a long time ago or, at the very least, left. Except she loved him. It didn't matter that this hurt, or that he'd embarrassed her by cheating. What mattered was that he'd apologized. That they'd shared a lifetime together and she wasn't ready to walk away from that. But would he feel the same?

"Well, it's true," Vivian said. "But I was going to say I think there is more to this than an affair. You have weathered those before. And given that Auggie was surprised about the boy, you normally would have been…more forgiving toward him. It makes me think… Is there something more you want to tell me?"

No.

Hell, no.

Juliette had promised to take the secret to her grave and she knew that once it was out, it would spread. She took a long sip of her drink. She shook her head, but a part of her wanted to tell her mom. To let go of the secret that had been a dark blot on her soul for too long now.

She wouldn't. But she wanted to.

"I won't push," Vivian said. "Remember when Musette came back from rehab the first time?"

She nodded. Where was her mother going with this? She had never been able to understand her sister's addiction or how she couldn't break it.

"I knew she was using again," her mom said. "I knew she was going to have to be the one to decide to stop, that it had to come from inside her, so I held my tongue. But watching her struggle and eventually fail was one of the hardest things I've ever done as a mother. Watching you try to deal with this is very similar. You look like you're about to implode and I don't know how to stop it."

"I—"

"Don't. Save the stories for the others you are telling them to. Just know I'll be here when it all falls apart."

She watched her mother walk away, wishing it were easier to tell her than it actually was.

# Treat Yourself with 2 Free Books!

**Sizzling Romance**

**Passionate Romance**

# GET UP TO 4 FREE BOOKS & 2 FREE GIFTS WORTH OVER $20

See Inside For Details

*Claim Them While You Can*

# Get ready to relax and indulge with your **FREE BOOKS** and more!

## Claim up to FOUR NEW BOOKS & TWO MYSTERY GIFTS – absolutely FREE!

Dear Reader,

We both know life can be difficult at times. That's why it's important to treat yourself so you can relax and recharge once in a while.

And I'd like to help you do this by sending you this amazing offer of up to FOUR brand new full length FREE BOOKS that WE pay for.

**This is everything I have ready to send to you right now:**

Try **Harlequin® Desire** books featuring the worlds of the American elite with juicy plot twists, delicious sensuality and intriguing scandal.

Try **Harlequin Presents® Larger-Print** books featuring the glamorous lives of royals and billionaires in a world of exotic locations, where passion knows no bounds.

Or **TRY BOTH!**

All we ask in return is that you answer 4 simple questions on the attached Treat Yourself survey. You'll get **Two Free Books** and **Two Mystery Gifts** from each series you try, *altogether worth over $20!* Who could pass up a deal like that?

Sincerely,

*Pam Powers*

Harlequin Reader Service

# Treat Yourself to Free Books and Free Gifts.

## Answer 4 fun questions and get rewarded.

### We love to connect with our readers! Please tell us a little about you...

|  | YES | NO |
|---|---|---|
| 1. I LOVE reading a good book. | ◯ | ◯ |
| 2. I indulge and "treat" myself often. | ◯ | ◯ |
| 3. I love getting FREE things. | ◯ | ◯ |
| 4. Reading is one of my favorite activities. | ◯ | ◯ |

### TREAT YOURSELF • Pick your 2 Free Books...

Yes! Please send me my Free Books from each series I select and Free Mystery Gifts. I understand that I am under no obligation to buy anything, as explained on the back of this card.

Which do you prefer?

☐ **Harlequin Desire®** 225/326 HDL GRAN
☐ **Harlequin Presents® Larger-Print** 176/376 HDL GRAN
☐ **Try Both** 225/326 & 176/376 HDL GRAY

FIRST NAME      LAST NAME

ADDRESS

APT.#      CITY

STATE/PROV.      ZIP/POSTAL CODE

EMAIL ☐ Please check this box if you would like to receive newsletters and promotional emails from Harlequin Enterprises ULC and its affiliates. You can unsubscribe anytime.

HD/HP-520-TY22

**BUSINESS REPLY MAIL**
FIRST-CLASS MAIL    PERMIT NO. 717    BUFFALO, NY

POSTAGE WILL BE PAID BY ADDRESSEE

**HARLEQUIN READER SERVICE**
PO BOX 1341
BUFFALO NY 14240-8571

NO POSTAGE
NECESSARY
IF MAILED
IN THE
UNITED STATES

# Nine

The day felt like it had gone on forever. Logan had been on Nantucket for three days and it felt like a lifetime. His father's point about Adler wasn't lost on him and he felt like the worst kind of douchebag ever. He'd avoided mingling with the rest of the family after the announcement had been sent to the press and gone for a walk on the beach to clear his head. He'd thought about texting Quinn, but honestly, he knew that as much as he wanted to see her, it wasn't the right thing.

For her.

It would be selfish, and right now he was trying to be a better man. But could he be? He'd always thought he was a Bisset 2.0, not as harsh and uncaring as his father about the companies and people he gobbled up in his quest to grow the business. He wanted to believe he was better than his father. But he wasn't. He'd been deluding himself.

He could say all he wanted that he had inherited his mother's grace and charm, but at the end of the day, he never opted to use those qualities. He always went for the kill in true Bisset style.

He shoved his hands through his hair. He should have skipped the wedding. He would be happier in his office working on deals, and just physically not being here would have been much better.

"Logan, wait up!"

He turned to see his oldest brother, Dare, calling him. Dare had an easy smile and though he was almost forty, seemed much younger. He had dark hair and their father's gray eyes. He was taller than their dad by an inch and always had an air of authority about him. He was the most levelheaded of all the siblings. As cantankerous as Logan's relationship with Leo and Zac was, his relationship with Dare was the opposite.

"Hey, sorry about leaving like that. I just…well, I've had enough of this," Logan admitted.

"Me too. I am happy for Adler, but this wedding has turned into the kind of situation I think we all would avoid if we could."

"Definitely. Also, I screwed up," Logan blurted.

"What? How?" Dare asked, falling into step beside him.

"I ruined one of Nick's business deals…it's a big one," Logan said. "Before you ask, I did it after I knew he and Adler were getting married. But news about it is about to break next week."

Dare put his hand on Logan's shoulder and squeezed. Unlike his father, who came in hot with consternation, Dare just got it. Got him. "I think that's not going to be a big deal. I mean now that Nick is our brother, surely business will change."

Logan shook his head. "It will matter to Nick. And I highly doubt that a man who was raised as Tad Williams's son is going to suddenly want to merge with Bisset Industries, if that's what you were thinking."

"I was. Actually, I have reached out to Nick and his family to see if I can open some kind of negotiation between our families," Dare said. "I've sat on some highly volatile committees in the senate, so I figured I was probably the only one who might be able to broker something between us."

"I doubt that anything you encountered in Washington will be as bad as this. I mean Dad and Tad hate each other. It's not just me who wants to beat the other guy. Dad has been trying to ruin Tad since he opened his business," Logan said.

"I wonder why," Dare said. "I could see if he'd realized that Tad's wife was his former lover, but I'm pretty sure Dad didn't know. So it has to be something else. Has he ever mentioned it to you?"

"No. I brought it up one time and he told me it was none of my business, so I dropped it," Logan said. He'd never seen his father react that way until the moment he'd seen Cora Williams in the room two days ago.

"I guess we'll have to wait and see what happens," Dare said. "Last night was totally crazy. Zac was funny. I'm glad he's back. I mean I know he's made a mess of things with Iris, but to be honest, I don't believe for a second the only reason he's with her is because she offered to invest in his yacht team."

"Me neither. That boy is in love. He'll figure it out. I've never seen him like this with a woman," Logan said. "Do you think it's just wedding vibes?"

"What do you mean?"

"That he thinks he's in love? That it's real?" Logan asked.

"I don't know," Dare said. "Before Mari fell in love with Inigo, I would have said that we Bissets weren't really meant for romantic relationships. We're better at friendships and just socializing. Making connections for business or politics. But now Zac…it seems genuine to me."

"Me too," Logan said, shaking his head. Quinn had been right when she'd said he liked to compete. And he knew from watching Zac this morning that love didn't leave room for winners. He doubted he'd ever be comfortable with that.

His phone vibrated in his pocket and Dare's beeped. "Family text."

"Another meeting," Logan said. "Honestly, I am done with these. I miss the days when the biggest scandal was Mari partying too hard and wearing skimpy clothing."

"I know she doesn't. She's loving that, after all the meetings to deal with the Mari problem, it's now about the Auggie problem. I never would have thought that Dad would cause this kind of scandal," Dare said. "After all the shit he gave us growing up, there is a part of me that is relishing it."

"Yeah. I'm torn. Part of me is glad he's human and can screw up like the rest of us, but I've always been the most like him, D. What if that's my future?"

Dare stopped him. "The fact that you're worrying about it tells me it won't be."

"I hope you're right."

Iris and Adler had left and Quinn had a few minutes to herself. She thought about texting Logan but in the end decided not to. Today at the golf club she'd almost dropped her guard. Almost let him back into her life. When he'd walked away, she'd been reminded that almost was all she could safely allow.

Instead she went back to her rental house and downloaded the footage she'd shot for the personal video for Adler and Nick. She poured herself a Fiji water and just stared at the video screen. She'd been filming weddings for the last four years and as she'd gotten closer to thirty, she'd started thinking about marriage. Maybe it was time to look for a guy and settle down.

Iris had been…well, making mistakes as she tried to find a man to be her life partner. Quinn didn't need a man to move her career forward. Not that Iris really did, either, but Quinn had noticed that her friend's peers had all moved on to marriage or motherhood. Iris had said she was too old to be single-girl-in-the-city and Quinn felt that sometimes. Especially when her younger crew members were going out and she just wanted to go home, change into her comfy clothes and binge watch something on Netflix…honestly, she usually chose *Gilmore Girls* or the latest rom com.

Her mom warned her that she was getting too settled in her eccentricities. Somehow her mother thought if she didn't find someone who got her weird side then she was going to be alone forever. That, to be honest, didn't sound all that bad, given how Juliette Bisset was dealing with the fallout of her husband's affair thirty-five years ago.

But at the same time, it would be nice to have someone to curl up with on cold nights and to talk about the latest gossip, and to feel just comfortable that they had each other. She shook her head.

Weddings did this. She knew it. She'd seen so many couples hook up at the destination weddings she'd filmed. Couples—like herself and Logan—who made no sense back home. Back in real life.

She needed to shake herself out of this mindset.

She knew part of the blame belonged squarely on Logan's broad shoulders. If he had gotten a little chubbier since college, if he'd somehow lost his charm or maybe become some kind of dull businessman, she could have resisted him.

Yeah, that was what she needed, she thought. He was just still…too sexy. Too attractive, and not just physically. And part of it was the challenge.

Her phone buzzed and she grabbed it, glancing down to see it was another news push from the wire. She scanned it and almost dropped her phone.

There was more to the story…

A nurse from a rural hospital had released a statement saying that Nick wasn't the only child born that day to Cora Williams, aka Bonnie Smith. Nick had a twin and the twin had been swapped just after birth with Juliette Bisset's stillborn baby boy.

Holy hell.

Was the nurse talking about Logan? She had to be. He and Nick were the same age. They didn't look alike but they were similar in height. And not all twins were identical. But still…

This couldn't be right. Why would the nurse wait so long to come forward?

Either way, this news was going to shatter Logan's world. He had always prided himself on being the best mix of his mom and dad. If Juliette wasn't his biological mom— Quinn wondered if she'd seen this story before the family. She started to text Logan but he needed to hear this in person so she raced over to his gran's house. There were a lot of cars in the driveway, which was to be expected given that Adler was getting married on Saturday.

Now that she was there, Quinn didn't want to just go into the house and blurt the news out. She texted Logan to meet her outside.

He was quick to respond.

Can't. Family meeting. Talk later.

This is important, she frantically typed.

I can't leave now. We can talk about sleeping together later.

Ok. It's about a news thing involving you not us hooking up.

Shit. But I can't talk now. Thanks for trying to warn me.

She realized that the news must have been delivered to the family. Quinn wasn't sure what to do. As the wedding video producer, this didn't affect her job. Sure, Nick and Adler would be upset, but the wedding details still needed to be filmed and everything needed to go on.

She'd focus on work.

She wasn't Logan's girlfriend, she told herself as she walked back to her house. But she was his friend. That hadn't changed over the years. And with his family in shambles, whether this story was true or just someone trying to make a quick buck off the Bisset and Williams names, didn't matter. Logan's sense of self was his rock. It was how he defined himself. And she knew, with his competitive nature, this kind of revelation would deeply affect how he viewed himself.

Quinn got together with her team and made sure that everything was ready for the wedding rehearsal and then the dinner afterward. Given all of the recent bombshells dropping about Nick and the Bisset family, she wanted to make sure her shoot went smoothly. That at least a small part of the weekend would go as planned.

She texted Iris to see if she'd talked to Adler, and Iris called her back.

"Hey, is something up?" Iris asked. "I'm with Adler. She and her dad are talking about the walk down the aisle. She wants to make sure that he plays the right song. Apparently, he wrote something new last night. Anyway, what's up?"

She debated telling Iris about the news story she'd read, but right now it was all unconfirmed and, for the first time since Quinn had gotten to Nantucket, Adler was doing just bride stuff. "Nothing. I was just checking on you both. Can I bring a camera-man over?"

Iris conferred with Adler and got the okay.

Quinn would do her job. If anything came of the news report then she'd be with Adler, the friend she'd actually come to Nantucket to celebrate and support.

The entire family, including Logan's grand-mother, were in the study as Carlton read them the wire story. Logan couldn't believe what he heard. He turned to his mom, as did everyone else, and her face was ashen. From what felt like a great distance, he heard Carlton say that he'd dispute the nurse's claim. But Logan knew that wouldn't be necessary.

The look on his mother's face told him the story was true.

"Jules?" his father said. "How is this possible? Nick and Logan don't look like each other. Is it true?"

She took a deep breath, wrapping her arms around her waist as she stood there in the corner next to the floor-to-ceiling bookcases lined with books that had been in his mother's family for generations. Though now Logan realized that wasn't his family. There was no part of him connected by blood to his mother's family, the Wallises. He was a Bisset, though. Maybe he should feel better about his cutthroat instincts because he might need them in this crisis.

But he didn't.

Logan hated every second of this and as much as he wanted to rage about this secret having been kept from him, he also needed all of the details. He wanted every bit of information so that it couldn't be used against him again.

"You know I was alone when I went into labor. Dare, you were here with Gran, and Auggie, you were away on a business trip. I met Bonnie— I mean… I guess she goes by Cora now. We were in the delivery room together. The hospital was very small and we were talking before the births. I was trying—"

"Skip to the part where you swap your dead baby for me," Logan said.

Everyone turned on him. He knew it had been a mean thing to say, but he wasn't interested in the long, drawn-out story with all the emotion. He was after facts. That was all he could handle at this moment.

"Don't be such a dick," Leo said.

"I'll be whatever I want, she's not my mom," Logan said. "Right? That's true, isn't it?"

August cursed and turned on him, but when their eyes met, Logan knew his father understood his anguish. His dad started toward him, but he just shook his head.

"Finish the story," Logan said, glancing back at his mom—at Juliette.

"My birth was quicker, and I was in the recovery room," Juliette said. "I was crying when Bonnie—I mean Cora—came back in. She was crying too. She had anticipated having one child but two was too many for her to handle. She'd gotten a partial scholarship to go back to school and thought she could manage with one child but with two she was going to have to skip college.

"I told her that my marriage would probably be over when my husband learned about the stillborn baby. The pregnancy had brought us back together. But I knew without that baby, your father and I would struggle to stay together."

"That's not—"

"Don't say it's not the truth, Auggie. We both know that we were barely keeping ourselves together as a couple then. Bonnie said she was going to have to give up one of the babies or maybe it would be better if she gave them both up," Juliette said.

"So you offered to raise one as our son," August said.

"I did. I also gave her money to support herself and get some help for the son she kept," Juliette said. "We swapped the bracelets and Logan became my son. I nursed you, you became my baby at that moment. I never thought of you as anything other than my son."

"So how did the nurse know?" Logan asked.

"She knew my son was stillborn and had gone away to do the paperwork. Even though Bonnie and I told her that she was mistaken, she knew the truth. I offered her a bribe, which she was reluctant to take but then Bonnie—I mean Cora—said that no one would ever find out, there were only the three of us. This way the boys would both be raised by mothers who could afford them and who wanted them. The doctor had already signed the paperwork and it was simply down to us filling it in. Bonnie took it from her and signed it. I thought that was it."

"You should have brought this to me," August said. "I could have—"

"What? What would you have done?" his mom demanded, but Logan could tell that she was angry and sad.

He got that. He felt the same way. But this lie was bigger than her or his father. This lie had, in one moment, stolen everything from him. Leo and Dare were on either side of him. Zac and Mari sat quietly across the room. They were all watching him and he felt like he was going to explode.

Logan stormed from the room. He heard his brothers calling for him to come back, but he just kept on walking and left his gran's—not his gran's, not really. He just left and got into his car and drove as far away from the house as he could go. That wasn't far, considering how Nantucket wasn't a huge island. But he needed to get away. He pulled into the parking lot for the ferry.

He pounded his fists on the steering wheel, but the angry energy inside him wasn't abated. He screamed and wanted to kick something. He needed a fight. He needed to figure out who he was because he'd been living a lie for thirty-five years. Everything he believed about himself was false. And he wished there were a way he could unknow that. Wished he could go back to being the man he'd been this morning.

But he'd never put much stock in dreams and he knew he was a man of facts. He had the truth now and he was the only one who could decide what to do with it. He was still a Bisset, thanks to his father's cheating ways, so he did the one thing he always fell back on: work and doing deals.

# Ten

Quinn played a hunch. When she was done filming Adler, she went to the ferry to wait and see if
Logan would show up. After about fifteen minutes,
she saw his black sports car with the vanity plate
Bsset1 pull into the lot. He drove to a corner. She
watched him pound his fists on the steering wheel.
Her heart broke.

She hated to see him like this.

She had no idea how to help him, if she even
could, but she also couldn't walk away. Couldn't let
him leave like this. The man she'd started to know
over the last day and a half was different from the
boy she'd known in college. Logan had changed,
matured into someone she liked.

She didn't want to see him do something rash. Make a decision out of anger that he'd regret.

Why did it matter to her? Quinn asked herself. She didn't bother answering.

It mattered because it was Logan and a part of her had always been vulnerable when it came to his happiness. She knew that she couldn't make him happy. She knew that as well as she knew he couldn't make her happy. But she had always tried.

Quinn walked over to the car. If he rejected her, told her to leave, then she would. But she had to try.

He stared at her for a second as she stepped up to the driver's-side window. She saw the tears in his eyes, and he didn't bother to wipe them away. He just hit the button to lower the window.

"You know?"

"I know," she said. "I'm sorry."

"Yeah, well, it is what it is," he said. His words weren't rageful or bombastic, as she'd expected after witnessing his outburst with the steering wheel, but they were subdued and almost numb.

"I got the news when I texted you. I didn't want to type that out. I thought you should hear it in person," she said.

"Yeah, thanks for that," he said.

"So, are you leaving?"

"I don't know. I just don't want to be around my family, and they are everywhere on Nantucket."

"Can I get in?" she asked.

"Why?" he asked. "I know you can't leave."

"I don't think you should either," she said. "And it's okay to tell me it's none of my business, but I think you need a friend and someone you can just be real with. You know I won't judge."

"I do know that," he admitted. "But you have to stay here. It's your job."

"I know. Stay with me. Don't do the wedding, don't see your family, if that's what you want. Stay with me like we just hooked up and you're on vacation. Take a few days to figure this out."

He gave a snort as he shook his head. "It's going to take a lot more than a few days to sort this out. But I think I would like to stay with you. Are you sure? I know you said one night only."

"I did. And I'm not sure what will happen between us. Come with me as a friend," she said.

He nodded. "Hop in."

She walked around the car and got in. He didn't bother to put it in gear but just rested his arms on the steering wheel and stared at the ferry port. If she'd just learned she wasn't who she thought she was, she'd be looking for a magic genie to make this all go away. But Logan had always been more practical. The kind of man who faced things head-on.

"I don't know what to do next," he said. "This isn't like a business hit where I can regroup and go after the person responsible…it's my mom…oh, God, Q, my mom isn't my mom," he said, putting his fore-head on the steering wheel.

She put her hand on his shoulder and squeezed. "She's still your mom. She raised you and she loves you. She's always going to be your mom."

"I get what you're saying but how can I look at her the same way?" Logan asked. "Everything's changed."

"It has. And there's no going back. I don' t know how you'll move forward, but I know you will."

"How? How do you know?"

"Because you're not someone to run away from a problem," she said.

He clenched his jaw and then nodded. "You're right. But I can't begin to think of a solution."

"Give yourself the day," she said.

"Just one day?" he teased.

"As many as you need. But I know you, Logan Bisset. You aren't one to wallow for long," she said.

He wasn't. It was funny that the woman he hadn't seen in over ten years would still know him so well, but he realized that he'd been more honest in his re-lationship with Quinn back in college than he'd been with any other person in a relationship since.

He knew part of it was that he'd been hurt when things had ended, and he'd decided never to allow someone to get close enough to make him feel like that again. And until today, when he'd learned of his mom's deceit, he hadn't. He'd protected himself well from feeling this kind of emotional pain.

Maybe Quinn was the only one to help him make sense of this and figure out how he was going to handle being a twin to a man he hated.

He hadn't forgotten about that. He'd been dwelling on the betrayal he felt with his mom, but Nick was his twin. How was that even possible? Nick was everything he hated.

"Don't think about anything else," Quinn said. "I can see it building in you."

"I don't think I can shut it off," he said. "Nick can't be my twin. I hate that man."

"He is," she said.

"How can you be so sure?"

"If he wasn't, you wouldn't be upset," she pointed out. "You don't know him outside of the boardroom. I think there is a lot more to him than you realize."

"Fuck. I don't want to like him," Logan said.

"You don't have to," Quinn said.

And that was enough. For this moment, he was okay with that.

Logan took a shower when he got to Quinn's house. He had his gym bag in the trunk of his car so he changed into a pair of basketball shorts and a T-shirt that he'd had in there. Quinn was on a conference call when he came out of the bathroom, so he just put on his headphones and went to sit on one of the loungers at the back of her house. He put on his sunglasses and tried to let the music distract him, but he couldn't control his thoughts.

They kept returning to that moment when he'd learned that his mom wasn't his mom. That he was a twin who had been given up by his biological mother moments after he was born. The one she didn't want. But Juliette had wanted him. She'd loved him. Raised him with so much love that he knew he'd be able to forgive her for keeping her secret. But it would be down the road.

For as long as he could remember, everyone had made him feel loved. His parents, his siblings, his friends. His life had been full of people who cared about him, and he couldn't help but wonder about Cora Williams, who had looked down at two babies and chose to get rid of him.

He'd never ask her. Hell, if he had his way, he'd never speak to her again. But that thought was there in the back of his mind.

He hadn't realized his fists were clenched until Quinn sat next to him and lifted one of them, slowly prizing his fingers apart. She pulled his headphones out of his ears with her other hand.

"What are you thinking about?"

"I'm trying not to think of anything but it's hard. I mean, why did Cora pick me to give away? Isn't that stupid of me?" he asked. "I mean…until a few hours ago I didn't even know she was my mom."

"It's not stupid," Quinn said. "It's natural to wonder that. Do you want to meet with her and talk to her?"

"No," he said. "She's nothing to me. If she hadn't given me to my—to Juliette—she would have put me up for adoption. Who knows who I'd be…"

"I do," Quinn said.

"You do?"

"Yes. You didn't just turn into a super-competitive, driven man by mistake. You were born that way, Logan. Even Dare has said you were determined to be your father's successor from a very young age."

"That's true. I guess there's no arguing I'm a Bisset through and through."

"There isn't. Just think how much harder this news would have been—"

He stopped her by putting his fingers over her lips. "Don't. I can't even bear to think of that. I hate that these thoughts are circling around in my mind. Like I don't know who I am anymore. When that's the one thing I've never questioned."

"I wish I could show you that you're still the same man," Quinn said.

"You can't. I'm always going to know there is a part of me that's a lie. You know I hate that the world knows it too," Logan said.

"I do. But don't think of it that way," she said.

"How else should I view it?" he asked. "The board will have questions."

"They might, but they know you're not going to suddenly be less effective…unless you decide that you no longer want to be," Quinn said. "This might not be what you want to hear, but perhaps you should look at this as a clean slate. As an opportunity to change the things you didn't like about yourself."

"Are you trying to tell me something?"

"Like what?"

"Is there something about me that's unlikable?" He wondered what she'd say. He knew he was too driven, too competitive, too determined to prove himself. This news wasn't suddenly going to make him less so. In fact, now he had more of a determination to make sure that no one questioned who he was.

"You know what I mean," she said. "You had mentioned cutting Nick out of a deal, maybe you will take a different approach in the future."

He doubted there would ever be a time when he and Nick weren't adversaries. Nick had been pretty clear that he considered Tad Williams his father, and rightly so. Tad had raised him. The same way Juliette had raised Logan.

Neither of their parents had been bad to them. Well, he couldn't speak for Nick, but from what he'd heard, Tad was an okay dad. "This is so complicated."

"It is," she said, shifting around to sit on his lap. He pulled her close, wrapping his arms around her.

"Do you have to leave soon?"

"I do. I'm taping Adler and Nick and then the wedding rehearsal," she said. "Then I have the rehearsal dinner… I think Zac is planning something special to make things up to Iris. Tomorrow I'll be busy all day but, starting Sunday, it's just you and me."

He wondered why he'd stayed on the island. He should have left; it would have made more sense. Quinn had work to do and couldn't just sit around with him. But he also knew he wouldn't have wanted that.

"Okay. I'll go with you to the rehearsal…will you be a guest or working the entire time?"

"I'll be working for a bit but then I'll be a guest," she said.

"I don't know how I'm going to face everyone."

"Like you always do," she reminded him. "You're Logan Bisset and everyone knows you rule the world. No one is going to pity you or feel sorry for you."

No one except himself. He felt sorry for himself that Juliette wasn't his biological mom. That he wasn't the man he'd always believed himself to be. But other people's pity wasn't something he felt comfortable with and neither was hiding out.

August was locked in the study with Carlton, and Juliette's mom hadn't left her side since Logan had left the house. Now they were in the kitchen, drinking a cup of tea, and Juliette's kids were all sitting at the table with her. No one had said a word since Michael had served them and left them alone.

Juliette knew she needed to do something to help her kids get through this but she had no idea what to say. She'd always been able to smooth over the mistakes that Auggie made. To figure out a way to guide her kids and keep them focused on moving forward. But this…she had had no idea.

"Has anyone heard from Logan?" she asked. It was on her mind. She hated that one of her sons was out there, alone. From that moment in the hospital when she'd held him he'd always been her son. She might have known the truth in her mind but her heart had always claimed Logan as her son. It didn't matter that he was a grown man and that he was upset with her. She was worried. She knew how he could be; he needed someone to talk to, but who would he discuss this with?

"I haven't," Leo said.

"He texted me to say he's with Quinn," Dare said. "Sorry I didn't mention it. I wasn't sure if he wanted anyone else to know."

"That's okay. I'm glad he's with her. Are they getting back together?" she asked.

"Mom. Don't act like everything is normal," Mari said. "We need to talk about this. I'm not going to pretend you haven't been keeping this a secret from us."

"I know things aren't normal, Marielle. I'm just

trying to keep from breaking into a million pieces. I'm trying to keep the rest of us together," she said.

"Well, it's not working," Leo said. "I can't believe you did that. I mean I'm glad Logan was raised with us, but you should have—"

"Should have what?" Mari asked. "Told Dad? Told us? That would have gone really great."

Mari's sarcasm was strongest when she was hurting, and Juliette realized that she'd done a lot of damage to the heart of their family. She hated to see the kids fighting and knew she was to blame.

"I'm sorry."

Dare got up and came to sit next to her, putting his arm around her shoulder and hugging her close. She hugged him back and felt tears burning her eyes as she did so. Her firstborn had always been a rock for her. She remembered the hot mess she'd been as a young mother, so unsure of herself. She'd screwed up a lot with Dare, but he'd turned out okay.

She had thought she'd done okay with all of the kids but this thing with Logan had proven otherwise. "No one was ever supposed to know."

"Secrets have a way of coming out," Vivian said. "No matter how well you think they are covered."

"Thanks, Mom. That helps."

Vivian shrugged and took a sip of her tea. "Don't snap at me. This was your secret, but as I see it, I don't think you could have done anything differently."

Juliette nodded.

She didn't either, but at the same time she regretted that she'd never said anything. Still, she'd justified putting it off. She'd been busy raising five kids, running her charities and keeping her marriage together. There had been a few moments when she'd let a thought creep in about that single mother who'd given her Logan, but it had always been a moment of gratitude that she had her wonderful son. Each of her kids was so different. So unique. And she loved them all. She didn't want to lose Logan now.

"I agree," Zac said. "Sometimes the secret gets bigger on its own. The circumstances change and you are stuck keeping quiet."

She looked over at her middle child. The one who was in a mess of his own making at the moment. "I never thought of Logan as anything other than my child."

Her other kids just nodded. They didn't need to hear this. Logan did. But he wasn't responding to her calls or her texts. She knew it would take time, but she didn't want to wait. She needed to make this okay. She needed her son back in her home, close to her, so she'd know he forgave her.

What if he never did?

"Does Nick know?" Leo asked. "I mean that he and Logan are twins?"

"I haven't been in touch with Adler," Juliette admitted.

"I talked to her a few minutes ago," Vivian said. "She sounded fragile. I offered for her to come over here or for me to go and see her but she said she needed to be alone."

"I'm so sorry. We should all be getting ready for the rehearsal. I feel like we've ruined her wedding."

"You have," Vivian said. "You and August have always played your little power games without thinking of the cost. We've barely had time to process the fact that August is Nick's father before your news comes out about Logan. It's like tit for tat."

"Mom," she said.

"It's true. It took you until last year to finally have a decent relationship with Mari because your anger at August got in the way."

"I never meant for it to end up like this," Juliette said. "Mari, you know I love you very much."

"I do," Mari said. "And Dad can drive us all up the wall at times. I'm not sure what you meant, Gran, but I'm pretty sure Mom didn't know about Nick and hadn't been plotting to one-up Dad with her secret about Logan. I think Mom just wanted another son to love. Maybe you should cut her a break."

Juliette was surprised that Mari had come to her defense. She wasn't sure she deserved it but Mari definitely understood her better than Vivian did. "Thank you, Mari. I'm so lucky to have you as my daughter."

"I know," Mari said with a wink. "This isn't a

great situation to be in or a great time to have this come out, but it has and I think we should remember that all Mom ever did was love us and raise us the best she could."

"I agree," Dare said. "We'll make sure we are there for Logan and he'll find his way back to us."

She hoped her kids were right. But having them in her corner, she felt luckier than she probably had a right to feel.

# Eleven

Logan could feel himself going down the moody, self-loathing, angry route as the afternoon wore on. Quinn left to do her job and he jogged to the grocery store, bought two bottles of Jack and dodged several paparazzi who weren't fooled by his sunglasses and Bisset Industries' baseball cap.

Go figure.

He gave them the finger as he left the grocery store and then gave them the slip at the hotel. Walking through the lobby of the hotel where a lot of his extended family and all of the wedding guests were staying wasn't his brightest decision, but it was safe to say that he wasn't firing on all cylinders at this point.

Reeling from his parents' revelations and wanting

nothing to do with reality wasn't like him. He went up to his hotel room, packed a suitcase and then realized he was going to have to walk back to Quinn's.

Why was he going back to her? He had originally gone to her place to spend time with her but she had to work. And, really, did he want Quinn to witness this? Hell, he was living through it and he didn't want to see it. He texted her that he'd gone back to his hotel in case she came home and worried.

Then he opened the bottle of Jack and poured himself a couple of fingers of whiskey. He sat on the couch in the junior suite he'd rented for the weekend.

He couldn't do it. Couldn't deal with the fact that the woman who'd raised him wasn't his mother. He knew the arguments—that she'd loved him, that she'd raised him—but at the same time she'd betrayed him.

It wasn't that he wouldn't have been able to deal with being adopted— Well, maybe he wouldn't have, but it would be different if he'd grown up believing that about himself.

But he hadn't.

At least Nick, that lucky bastard, had always known Tad wasn't his father.

There was a knock on the door and Logan ignored it. He wasn't really in the mood to do anything but drink until he was numb.

The knock came again. "I know you're in there. Open up."

It was Quinn.

Images of the two of them from the other night on the beach danced through his mind. She'd always been too…he wouldn't say good for him, but just too nice for him. She cared about other people, something he'd always struggled with. Hell, now that he knew his biological mother had given him up minutes after his birth, he might have his explanation. He hadn't inherited her kindness gene because they weren't related by blood.

"Logan."

"Go away. I'm wallowing."

"No," she said. "People are coming off the elevator. Let me in."

Her words were low, terse, and he could sense she was getting angry at him. Angry Quinn he could handle. A fight might be good. He didn't want to deal with Caring Quinn. The woman who looked at him and saw past the façade of confidence and arrogance to the man beneath.

He opened the door and glanced down the hall to the area by the elevator, which was empty.

"Where'd they go?"

"Must have decided not to get off on this floor," she said, pushing past him. She had on a silk bomber-style jacket and a tank top with a pair of skintight black jeans. She had headphones around her neck and her smartphone in her hand.

"Are you supposed to be working?"

"I am working. We're taking a ten-minute break

before I do an interview with Adler and Nick," she said. "I was worried about you. Are you drinking?"

"I am."

"Stop," she said. "That's going to make you feel worse."

She walked into the suite, opened the minibar, took out a bottle of Diet Coke and then turned to face him. He'd followed her, plopped back down on the couch and poured himself another glass of whiskey. "Tomorrow."

"Tonight. You shouldn't be drinking alone. Zac's got his own issues to deal with but surely you can call Dare and Leo."

"No, I can't, Ace. I don't want them to know that I'm…" He stopped. Any word that he could use to describe what he was feeling right now, he didn't want to say and he definitely didn't want either of his brothers to see him that way.

"Logan."

"Quinn."

He knew she was trying to help, and in a way she was. She was distracting him from the dark spiral his mind was all too willing to take him down. Never in his entire life had he been unsure of himself like this. There were times when he had used bravado to convince himself that he was okay. But he'd always been confident. Very certain about his place in the world.

And now he wasn't.

"Please don't do this. I have to go back and finish filming and I don't want to leave you this way."

"I'll be fine. I'm an adult, remember?"

She smiled. "I do. I seem to recall you saying if you have to tell someone that fact then maybe you're not as mature as you think you are."

"A very wise man," he said, recalling the conversation they'd had back in college. "Or just a guy trying to sound clever so he could score."

"You failed," she reminded him.

"That was just my opening salvo," he said. "I got there in the end."

"You did," she said. Her phone started vibrating in her hand and she glanced at the screen. Her brow furrowed and she tapped out a message before looking back at him.

The look on her face made him put down the whiskey. She was worried, and not just a little bit. She had that nervous look that he'd often seen on other's faces when he walked into a boardroom during a corporate takeover.

He stood and faked a smile the way his mom—Juliette—had taught him. "I'm fine. Go work."

He walked her to the door of his suite, kissed her and then opened the door and nudged her on her way. He'd be fine because he never wanted anyone to look at him that way again.

Quinn's team was all back by the time she walked into one of the small breakout rooms where they would be filming the interview with Adler and Nick. When they were done, she and her team were going to review the footage. They'd set up a small editing suite in a hotel room on the same floor for that purpose. Since the wedding would be broadcast live, all of the stuff they'd shot so far was going to be used as an intro and B-roll stuff.

"I like what we have. For now it almost seems as if the scandal isn't an issue, which I think you want us to keep that way, right?" Joe the editor said. "The network said to keep it classy. I think they are worried that we'll seem too tabloid-y."

"I got the same sort of warning from my boss," Quinn replied. "Let's send them the interview once we're done filming it and I've approved the cut—so they can see what we're doing. That it's tasteful and all that. Our viewers are mostly tuning in to get ideas for the own weddings."

"Sounds good. I'll start working on the golf footage from this morning and the clambake from last night. You got some good stuff with the different guests. Also can we use Toby Osborn's song and the footage of Nick and…the other dude singing?"

"I have Abby working on that. She's talking to licensing—we might have to just use license-free music. We should know before tomorrow. Just go ahead and edit it as if we can use the songs for now."

"I will."

Joe left and Quinn went over to the love seat and

checked the lighting with her camera guy before Nick came in. His hair was tousled, as if he'd been running his hands through it, and that wasn't something he normally did. "You okay?"

"Yeah. I guess you heard that Logan is my twin," he said without preamble. "I don't want to discuss that right now. I think we can just say that I found out who my biological dad was and it hasn't changed the way I feel about Adler. Will that be okay?"

"Yes. Honestly, Nick, whatever you want to say will be fine. And we can cut it out if you don't like it. I just think that it might be nice for you two to be able to control the narrative here."

"Me too," he said. "It would be so nice to control something at this point. I swear, if one more secret about my birth comes to light, I'm not going to be able to handle it."

"Yes, you will," Adler said as she came into the room. She was dressed in a jumpsuit that was slim-fitting on top and then flared out into palazzo trousers. She had her hair pulled back in a low chignon with tendrils framing her heart-shaped face. She looked beautiful and composed, but her eyes betrayed her and her lips trembled a little when she tried to smile.

Nick nodded and then just pulled her into his arms. Quinn turned away to give them privacy but also looked over at her camera man to make sure he was filming. This was the kind of moment their

viewers loved. Those little behind-the-scenes inti-
macies between the bride and groom.

Nick cleared his throat and Quinn turned back
around, smiling. "I think we're ready."

They both had their microphones on and took
their seats. Quinn would be off camera asking questions to lead the interview and direct them so they
stayed on topic.

"No wedding goes to plan, and yours has had a
few bumps. Do you want to discuss that?"

Adler smiled and this time she exuded confidence
as she held on to Nick's hand. "Well, Nick always
knew that Tad Williams wasn't his biological father,
but we just found out that he's the son of business ty-
coon August Bisset. My aunt is married to August,
so it was a bit of shock all around."

"It was surprising, but it changes nothing between
me and my parents. I'm still the man I always was
and I think you still like me, right?" Nick looked
down at Adler and smiled. It was a sweet moment.

"Yeah, I do," she said.

"Can't wait until you say that tomorrow," Nick
said.

"Me neither," Adler responded.

"Tell us some of the ways that you're incorporat-
ing family into your ceremony," Quinn said, happy
that they had at least addressed the scandal and then
moved past it.

"Adler's dad wrote a song for us that he'll be performing at dinner after the ceremony and, actually, last night I got to duet with him at the bonfire," Nick said.

"Yes. Dad's music will be a big part of the ceremony and my mom wrote a song about me before she died that my dad's girlfriend is going to perform at the ceremony," Adler added.

Adler was really touched that Toby's girlfriend, Sonia, had offered to perform it. It was going to be a nice way to honor the memory of Adler's mom as part of the ceremony.

Quinn asked them a few more questions and as they talked she couldn't help but look for signs that Logan and Nick were twins. But it was hard to see it on the surface. Obviously they both looked very different. Logan was blond and a few inches shorter than Nick. But they both had that square jaw, like August, and they both were men who went after what they wanted.

It was easy for Quinn to see how much Nick wanted Adler, how much he loved her. And her mind drifted to Logan. Did he see her that way?

Adler thought Nick had handled himself really well during the interview. But that had just been the two of them. Now that she was at the rehearsal with all of the people responsible for the scandals that kept dropping she was having a moment where she wanted to throw a massive bridezilla fit or just sit in a corner and cry. She was so ready for this weekend to be over—something she'd never thought she'd feel about her wedding.

Her aunt Jules had tried to call her, but Adler had shut her down. She couldn't deal with any of the Bisset family right now. Mari had left a voice-mail saying she was there if she needed to talk, but Adler didn't think raging at her cousin about how her parents were the worst people on the planet was going to really help.

Iris wasn't too happy about having the fact that she'd paid Zac to be her date revealed to the world, but her friend had found her peace with it. Adler wished she could likewise find peace with the revelations about Nick. But she knew part of her was looking at Nick differently now.

He was her touchstone. Her safety net. The love of her life. But now he was different. He might have said in the interview that nothing had changed, but it had. He wasn't speaking to his mom, which only added to the tension of the rehearsal. And for her part, Adler was ignoring Aunt Jules.

"Hey," Quinn said, pulling her aside. "I get that you're mad at Juliette, but I need some kind of footage where you aren't glaring at her or Nick's mom. I think it might be better if we just have you and Nick and maybe your dad and the bridal party for the filming. I know how difficult this is for you—"

"Do you?" Adler snapped. "My dream wedding

has turned into one crazy-ass scandal after another and I'm supposed to smile and act like nothing has happened."

"I know it's hard. I'm sorry. But I have to film this. And I want to do it in a way that you'll be happy with," Quinn said, turning away. "Take a few minutes while we set up for some different angles and then we can try again."

Adler realized she was turning into a bridezilla. "Q!"

She ran after her friend and hugged her. "I'm sorry. I'm just losing it."

"I know. It's not personal. I have to have something, and if we use what I've filmed so far, you're not going to like it."

"Fair enough. Give me a minute to talk to Aunt Jules and Cora," Adler said.

"Okay. Want me to send Iris over so you're not alone?" Quinn asked.

"No. I need to do this by myself," she said.

Nick was standing in a group with the groomsmen, which included her cousin Zac, who had filled in last moment for a no show. Nick's brothers and father were with them. August Bisset hadn't come to the rehearsal, which Adler was glad about. Cora was talking to Olivia, and Aunt Jules was over by Mari and Iris.

She took a deep breath. She couldn't let the actions of these two women more than thirty years ago ruin her wedding. And she knew they didn't want them to.

"Aunt Jules? Cora? Could I have a word with you both?" Adler asked.

Olivia and Mari both looked at her, their eyes wide. But the older women just nodded, and Adler turned to walk toward the back of the church where they could have some privacy.

"Adler, let me—" Cora started once they were out of earshot of the others.

"Please don't, Cora. Let me just say this. I'm not happy with either of you right now. A part of me knows that's unfair, but it's how I feel," she said. "You both seem angry with each other as well, and since this wedding is being televised, I think we need to clear the air before we let them film another minute."

"I agree," Aunt Jules said.

"Of course, Adler, it's your special day and Nick's. I don't want to ruin it for either of you," Cora said.

Both of them were so contrite, quiet and almost sad that she felt wrong saying anything, but she knew she had to. "Thank you both for agreeing. The thing is, I am struggling to forgive you both for what you did. I know I'm not the one who needs to forgive you but there it is. I hate that you both kept this a secret until my wedding weekend. Even the fact that you feel bad for what you did isn't enough.

"Nick isn't himself. The paparazzi are swarming

around him. And my dad, who is finally clean and in an actual healthy relationship, is contemplating doing something outrageous to draw the spotlight off of Nick's parentage. This isn't right."

"I'll speak to Toby," Aunt Jules said.

"That's not the point," Adler said. "I can't figure out how to not be angry with you."

"Don't," Cora said. "You're completely justified in being upset. We both are as well. We aren't going to magically all form some family. Juliette and I will stay in the background and give you space to be the center of attention."

"Yes," Aunt Jules added. "This is your chance to celebrate your love for Nick and the life you two are building. No one wants to intrude on that."

Adler nodded. She wasn't getting the closure she needed but Cora had been right when she'd said it was too soon for any of them to really achieve that. They would just all make the best of the situation. "Thank you."

"You're welcome," they both said at the same time.

Aunt Jules reached out to hug her and Cora looked like she wanted to as well. In that moment, Adler realized that as much as this weekend might have been for her, it wasn't anymore. She was caught in the middle of two warring families and she either had to figure out how to broker peace or decide if she wanted to peace out.

She hugged them both and noticed Nick watching

them. He lifted one eyebrow at her, the way he did when they were at a party and he wanted to make sure she was okay. She tried to smile but she realized she wasn't just angry at these two women. She was also mad at him.

# Twelve

Logan was standing by the window in the hall-way outside the ballroom when Quinn found him as she left the rehearsal dinner. She had decided to wear a cute sundress with wide shoulder straps and a flared skirt that made her feel very feminine. Like she wanted to twirl. That was precisely the reason why she usually wore jeans.

She'd expected Logan to cave and show up, so had been disappointed when she hadn't seen him there. She'd gotten dressed up for herself and her friends, not for him, or so she'd told herself when she'd left her bungalow. But a part of her knew she wanted to see him. Wanted to find a bit of the romance that was swirling around the events at the Nantucket Hotel despite the fact that the past was rearing its ugly head.

She'd stepped out of the hotel ballroom as Zac got up on the stage to sing to Iris, probably well on his way to winning her back. The Bisset men knew how to bring out the romance when it suited them. And after today, when she'd talked to Adler and Nick and Logan about all the different emotions that the news of August and Cora's affair and the results stirred up, she just wanted to be with Logan.

She wanted to be with this man who was dressed in a Tom Ford suit and staring out the window like he'd lost his center and didn't know how to find it.

The look on his face as he stood there stirred all those feelings she'd been denying he made her feel. All that love and need and the desire to wrap him in her arms and do whatever she could to soothe the savage beast inside him. Except that she knew he didn't want to be soothed. He wanted to savage something. Someone. She wouldn't let him ruin Adler's wedding and she knew Logan well enough to know that he wouldn't want to do that.

He was probably readying himself for something she knew he'd regret after the fact. Like stealing the business deal out from under Nick. He always lashed out when he was angry and took the revenge he thought he deserved. But when the time passed and he had a moment to breathe and reflect, he always regretted it.

Had he changed enough for her to feel safe being with him?

"Quinn."

He'd turned to her while she'd been ruminating on whether she should stay or leave. The anguish in his eyes coupled with the way that suit fit him just brought her to her knees. He looked strong, sexy and so alone, that she couldn't help walking over to him.

She just stood there trying to tell herself she wasn't falling for him while knowing it was a big lie. There was no way she could resist Logan like this. She knew it, so why wasn't she wanting to run for the ferry and go back to the mainland to get as far from him as she could?

She didn't want to.

She liked her life; she wasn't going to pretend she didn't. But she wanted Logan. She craved the feelings that only he stirred in her. And he'd changed. She felt it all the way to her soul. He was a better man now.

And…

The biggest reason of all…

He needed her.

She saw it in his eyes and in his body when he reached one arm out to her. He needed her to come to him. And she did.

She didn't question it or try to justify it.

This wasn't a thinking thing.

This was a feeling thing.

This was a Logan thing.

This was a Quinn pretending it would be okay thing.

She nestled against his side, tipping her head to look up at his profile. He went back to staring out the window and she shifted her gaze to see what he was looking at. Then her breath caught in her throat.

August and Juliette stood in the hotel parking lot. From this distance, it was hard to see what was happening, but it looked like they were arguing.

"Oh, Logan."

"It's got to be about me. All her life she had the high ground in arguments with him. She's always put the family first, always put her smile on and stood next to him regardless of what he'd done and now…me."

"That's between the two of them. No matter how it feels right now, she'll still always put the family first," Quinn said. "Come on. Come with me and dance and forget about this."

"I can never forget this, Ace. This is who I am," he said. "I don't want to dance and smile. I'll probably take a swing at Nick because without him we'd never be here."

"I'm not sure that logic works," Quinn pointed out gently.

"I don't care. I know it makes no sense, but I don't want to be here, I don't want to know the truth or see it on everyone's face. I want to go back to the way it was before this stupid wedding," Logan said.

Quinn realized that he wasn't going to be okay. She thought time would heal him, but this cut seemed too deep.

"Want to go to your room?" she asked.

"Can you come with me?" he asked. "Are you done working?"

"Yes," she said.

He took her hand in his and led her down the hall to the bank of elevators. His parents entered through the side door as they approached. She slipped her hand under his arm and squeezed.

"Logan."

"Dad. Juliette," he said to them, and punched the elevator call button with more force than was necessary.

"You don't call your mother by her first name," August said.

Quinn was struck by how he might have been arguing with Juliette in the parking lot but he had her back with Logan.

"She's not my mom, is she?" Logan asked.

Tears rolled down Juliette's face and August lunged for his son. But Juliette held him back and Quinn grabbed Logan's arm, forcing him down the hall, away from his parents.

Losing Logan wasn't something that Juliette ever thought she'd have to face, but as her son walked away, she knew she had. August, even after all his anger in the parking lot, turned to her and, for the first time in a very long time, he didn't seem like he was holding part of himself back.

"I'll make him—"

"You can't make him," she said. "I never thought this would come out."

"You told me the truth always does," he reminded her. His tone was gentle; one he didn't use very often.

This was the man she'd fallen in love with. Not the one who could charm the room or who could broker billion-dollar deals before breakfast, but the man who had a deep well of empathy and used it sparingly. Just on a special few.

"I wish I'd told you, but we weren't in a good place," she admitted.

"It's my fault," he said. "Your actions were your own but they were motivated by me and the way that I was at that time. If I'd never had an affair and left you alone, maybe our son wouldn't have been still-born. There are a million possibilities, but we are on the path that you and I have made. We have to trust that we raised Logan well enough that when he calms down from this betrayal, he'll come back to us."

"Us?" she asked. "He's not mad at you, is he?"

"I think it's safe to assume everyone knows I'm the one to blame. If I hadn't been so busy trying to prove I was the biggest, baddest asshole in the room and been more present with the family…maybe things would be different," he said. "I have to be honest, Jules, I anticipated a lot of things happening this weekend, but not what's actually come about."

She gave him a weak smile. "Same. How ironic is it that I end up in the same delivery room as your lover?"

"I think fate was playing tricks on us. Logan and I have both been in the same room with Nick and Tad, and I have to tell you those two men are nothing alike. I can see your influence in Logan's upbringing. Hell, Leo's just like him."

Juliette nodded. She knew her husband was trying to make her feel better and though her heart ached to go after Logan, she had to admit that Auggie was helping.

Someone cleared his throat. They glanced toward the ballroom where the rehearsal dinner was being held and saw Dare.

Her eldest son. She'd screwed up so much when she'd been a new mom, she knew she should be grateful he'd turned out as well as he had. A politician known for his fairness and bipartisan cooperation, he was truly the best of her and Auggie.

"Yes?" Auggie asked.

"Adler needs you, Mom. She's not sure she's going to go through with the wedding and just told Nick in front of the entire dinner party," Dare said.

"Oh, dear. This just keeps getting worse. Musette is probably cursing me from the afterlife," she said, rushing past Dare and into the room where Adler was just walking away toward the kitchens in the back.

Juliette wove her way through the partiers, trying to catch up to her niece. Cora, Olivia and Mari were right behind her as well. They didn't have to go far. Adler had only made it to the staff hallway and was leaning against the wall, tears streaming down her face.

Juliette went to her and pulled her into her arms. Adler resisted for a moment but then buried her head in Juliette's shoulder and cried.

"It's okay." She just rubbed Adler's back and kept murmuring to her.

"I think we just need to take a breath," Cora said.

"I agree," Juliette said, looking at the other woman. They shared so much but were both essentially strangers. Mari looked at her and Juliette nodded, indicating she should come and take care of Adler.

Then she pulled Cora aside. "I think we need to get the two of them in a room to talk this through. Can you try to talk to Nick?"

"Yes. I can. I know he's not handling August being his father very well and I'm afraid his dislike of Logan hasn't really helped with the other news," Cora said.

"I know. Logan's not even talking to me. But we can remind Adler and Nick that they love each other," Juliette said.

"Will that be enough?" Cora asked.

"I don't know. Frankly, I'm out of ideas. Do you have any other suggestions?" she asked the other woman.

Cora shook her head, chewing on her bottom lip. "Nick adores Adler. I think I'll try to remind him what's important. Maybe you can do the same with Adler?"

"I will. We can't let them go to bed until they have made up," Juliette said.

"Agreed. Olivia, come with me," Cora called to her daughter. "I'll text Mari after I've talked to Nick."

"Sounds good," Juliette said. The two women didn't have each other's cell numbers.

Cora and her daughter left, and she turned to Adler and Mari. Adler's mascara hadn't run, but her nose was red and her eyes were still watery. "Why did I think I wanted to get married to him?"

"Because you love him," Mari said. "And he loves you. Don't forget men can be dumb sometimes…not saying women can't too, but Inigo has done some really stupid stuff. Our wedding is stressing me out and it's just going to be a small affair in Texas at his family's estate."

"That's right. Mari's situation is a good example of this," Juliette added. "This wedding is a party to celebrate the couple that you are with your friends. All of these events are just icing on the cake. Right

now, it seems like the cake tipped over in the back
of the truck and the icing is smeared and pieces of
cake are showing through, but the cake is still good.
You and Nick are still good. He's still the man you
fell in love with."

"Is he?"

"Yes. He's struggling and you're nervous because
nothing is going according to the plans you've made.
But the two of you are meant for each other, Adler,"
Juliette reminded her. "If you want to send everyone
home and cancel the film crew, then we will do it.
But I feel like you'll regret letting Nick go."

Adler appreciate her aunt and cousin trying to re-
assure her, but this wasn't something either of them
could understand. Their fiancé hadn't turned from
a sweet great guy into someone they didn't recog-
nize. Nick was out of control. He'd been drinking
way more than he normally did since he'd learned
that August was his biological father.

And the thing with Logan had really sent him into
a spiral. She was trying to be understanding, trying
to give him the benefit of the doubt and let him have
space to come to terms with it, but they were getting
married tomorrow.

There wasn't time for him to fall to pieces and
put himself back together the way he needed to. She
needed him here and present.

"Darling girl, what can I do? Do you need me to

go and talk some sense into Nick? Do something out-rageous so everyone gives you both some space?" her dad said as he came in to the hall. Sonia was behind him, wearing her trademark long flowy skirt and her bangles, which jangled as she moved.

"Don't do any of that, Dad," Adler said.

"Cora is talking to Nick," Aunt Jules added. "I'm sorry for my part in this, Adler. I wish… I just wish this wasn't happening now."

Adler took a deep breath. She wasn't mad at her aunt anymore. She was more upset by how Nick was acting and changing. Jules had done the best she could with the hand she'd been dealt. The coming-out timing could have been better for Adler, but she wasn't going to worry about her aunt right now. She was worried about Nick.

He wasn't acting like himself and seemed to have completely shut down on her. She'd wanted to force him to show her what he was feeling, and her out-burst hadn't been planned, but once the words had left her mouth and he'd let her go, she was begin-ning to wonder if this wasn't what she should have done yesterday.

Marriage was a big step. Her father had been mar-ried so many times that she'd lost count. Not really, but it felt like that. He'd had eight wives, and that didn't count the number of live-in partners he'd had while she'd been growing up. For her, marriage was a one-time thing.

Adler had thought that Nick got that. That he was on the same page as she was. But tonight…when he'd let her walk away and hadn't followed her…well, she wondered if he was ready for a life with her.

"Everyone is wondering what's going on," Sonia said.

"Let them," her dad said. "Adler's what matters."

"I agree, but I thought if we went out there and rocked the house, maybe they'd forget about Adler for a while and that will give her some time to get things worked out," Sonia said. "Unless you're not working things out?"

Sonia had reddish blond hair that was shot with gray and warm, brown eyes. From the moment she'd started dating Toby, Sonia had been caring and motherly toward Adler. That was something she'd really appreciated, and right now her suggestion sounded perfect. "Can you do that, Dad? It would give me a moment to breathe and think of what I should do next."

"Of course I can, darling girl," Toby said. "I'll do whatever you need."

"Thanks, Dad," she said, hugging him. "Go rock out and I'll… I guess I need to find Nick."

"Not yet," Mari said. "Cora's texting me after she talks to him."

Adler took a deep breath as her dad and Sonia left, and then turned to her cousin. "If his mom can't get through to him, then no one will be able to."

"I think everyone just wants to bring the focus back to the wedding," Aunt Jules said.

"I know you do," Mari said. "Ad, listen, you've been out of the spotlight for a while and I'm happy to give you some tips to help you manage it."

"Like what?" she asked.

"Don't listen to her. She was very antagonistic with the press, and had to resort to extreme measures to make them go away," Aunt Jules said.

Adler remembered all those angry photos of Mari giving the camera the finger and more than one lawsuit over when her cousin had verbally assaulted paparazzi after it was revealed she'd had an affair with a married man.

"It made them go away for a while," Mari said. "The thing is we need someone not related to the wedding to do something over the top, you know?"

"I do, but it seems like I'd be inviting bad karma to wish that on someone else," Adler said. "My dad has offered but he's finally…"

"I know," Mari said. "Karma is a bitch and when it comes for you, there is no dodging it, right, Mom?"

Juliette looked at her daughter for a minute. "I hadn't thought of it that way, but you are right. Payback doesn't always come the way you expect it to. I mean I wanted Auggie to understand how betrayed I'd felt every time he cheated on me and I guess hiding the fact that Logan wasn't my biological son did that."

Adler shook her head. She wasn't going to wish anything bad on anyone. She didn't want to add to the mess they were all currently stuck in. And while her aunt and cousin were distracting, her heart ached at the fact that Nick hadn't come after her or even tried to find her. Was there any hope for the two of them?

# Thirteen

Logan knew he should be alone, but Quinn had followed him up to his room. He was so close to punching something. Punching the wall would be good. It would give him the satisfaction of hitting as hard as he could as well as some resulting pain, which he could channel his anger toward.

He couldn't believe what he'd said to his mom. He'd known how badly those words would wound her and had chosen them for that purpose, but he hadn't expected to feel that backlash of pain, guilt and shame.

"Logan, are you okay?"

Quinn's voice was softer than it normally was, as

if she knew he was a wounded animal and trying to soothe him. That only served to make him angrier. He didn't want to be soothed or pitied. Yet everything this weekend was forcing him into a position that demanded that.

"Yeah."

"Liar," she said, teasing him.

He didn't know if she felt like he was more able to handle it or if she was scrolling through a bunch of ways to treat him, trying each to see which one worked.

"You're right," he said, pivoting on his heel to face her. He shoved the sides of his jacket back and put his hands on his hips. "I am lying. I'm not okay. I just said the worst possible thing to my mom, and you know what? I would say it again. I almost wish she'd let my dad hit me because I'm mad at him too. And I know I'll regret all of this later, but for this moment I just feel…like I'm going to explode. Like I need to explode because maybe then I won't feel so fragile."

Quinn kicked off her high heels as she walked over to him. The skirt of her dress swooshed with each step she took. Her reddish-brown hair had been curled and swung around her shoulders. She tipped her head to the side as she got closer, narrowing one eye and studying him. She took his tie in her hand and tugged on it.

He stayed where he was for a moment before he gave in and let her pull him toward her.

"Fighting never helps," she said. "But maybe you need a competition to distract you."

Yes. "What'd you have in mind?"

"A little game of teasing. First one who cracks loses."

"Or wins," he said. "Depending on how they crack."

"Exactly. You game?" she asked.

"Are you sure, Ace?"

"Scared you can't keep it together?" she asked. "I mean you know what's underneath these clothes and it might be too much temptation for you."

He needed this. Needed her more than he'd realized until this very moment. "Oh, I think I'm up to the challenge. What are the rules?"

"Anything goes," she said. "First one to ask for something from the other one loses."

"Fair enough," he said, putting his arm around her waist and lifting her off her feet. He brought his mouth down on hers, not hard but just forceful enough to let her know he was here for this. Here for her. He kissed her long and deep, and shoved the thoughts of everything and everyone else out of his head.

It was just him and Quinn and that big king-size bed behind him. Win or lose, he knew he needed nothing more than this.

Sex wasn't a solution—or was it? Would it be his salvation? None of that mattered at this moment. He felt her fingers on the back of his neck, slowly caressing her way to his ear. She traced the outer shell and then pinched the lobe and he felt a jolt all the way down his body as he hardened.

She flicked the lobe of his ear with her finger again and he fought to keep from groaning out loud.

The stakes got a little higher as he realized how many of his turn-ons Quinn knew and was willing to exploit. She pulled her mouth from his, kissing his jawline and then sucking the lobe of his ear into her mouth and biting on it. Then she pulled back and whispered into his ear.

Her breath was hot, her words steamy. "Remember that time you and I were in the hot tub on winter break in Aspen? And you were determined that we wouldn't do it while others were around? And I ended up on your lap, sitting and talking to our friends while stroking your cock?"

He hardened a little bit more. As if he could have forgotten that.

"I remember that I had my hand in your bikini bottoms and my finger deep inside you. And you kept rocking against my touch as if you couldn't get enough."

She nipped at his ear again. "That was a nice night."

A nice night, indeed.

He turned away from her, shrugging out of his suit jacket and walking slowly across the room to hang it up on the valet in the corner. He felt the weight of her gaze on him as he moved. Knew she liked the way he looked in a suit and that this one fit him to a tee.

He turned back around and she waggled her eyebrows at him. "I do love a sharp-dressed man."

"I know," he said. "And I like that dress you're wearing. You don't wear them very often, but you have great legs."

"Thank you," she said, turning slightly from side to side, letting the skirt swish around her legs. "I love dresses, but no one takes me seriously when I wear one."

"I can see why," he said. "All I want to do is take *you*."

"That's because you're always thinking about sex," she said, reaching up underneath her skirt. A moment later her panties dropped to the floor and she stepped around them.

He groaned as he felt himself hardening even more. She looked so sophisticated and together, and now he knew she wasn't wearing underwear. It was almost too much and he had to force himself not to grab her and shove his hands up underneath that skirt.

"Care to dance?" he asked. He was going to take this slow and easy. He was playing this game to win;

he always played to win. And tonight, he could use a tick mark in the W column.

"What'd you have in mind?"

"I'm not sure. Let me see what I have on my playlist," he said. He was stalling for time, trying to pull himself back from the edge.

Quinn felt like she might have won that round by dropping her panties. She knew Logan was just taking a breather, and she could use one too. She hadn't expected that just watching him walk across the room would get her so hot. To be fair, that kiss had started the slow melt inside her. She was hot and horny and ready for him. But she also knew this wasn't a competition she was prepared to lose. Logan needed a good, long fight, not some easy win.

While she knew she'd feel like a winner either way, Logan needed this score. She wanted it for him. And, to be honest, for them both. But there was a part of her that wanted the win too. She needed to know that these emotions swirling around inside her since they'd had sex on the beach weren't one-sided.

She wanted to know that he was starting to think about her as more than a weekend sex romp. When she went back to real life on Monday, she was afraid she didn't want this to end.

She heard applause and then the riff of electric guitar, and shook her head. "Shake For Me." It was like playing dirty. She loved Stevie Ray Vaughan;

the first time she'd danced with Logan this song had been playing. They'd been at a party at a frat house and one of the Texas boys had put it on.

Quinn threw her head back and laughed, remembering the smells of beer spilled on the floor from the keg, and smoke, and then Logan's expensive, woodsy cologne as he'd come over to her and asked her to dance.

He winked at her. "Will this do?"

"Bring it, boy," she said, slowly dancing her way over to him. She put her hands on his ass, grinding against him to the music as he put his hands on her waist and did the same. Logan had a natural rhythm and while some men might struggle to feel comfortable in their skin when they danced, he didn't.

When the chorus came, Logan started singing along, his voice low and gravelly, mimicking Stevie Ray, inviting her to shake like wild.

And she did. Shaking for him as they both danced to the song. Each brush of his body added fuel to the fire burning inside her. His erection nudged her stomach and she wished she was wearing a pair of jeans and a tank top instead of this dress. But the dress worked.

She pushed her leg between his, felt the strength of his thigh as he cupped her butt, drawing her up his thigh and then letting her slide back down. The next song on the playlist was "Pride and Joy." Another classic *Double Trouble* song. And actually, her favorite. They'd had sex the first time while this was playing in the background. It had been three weeks after that first dance.

He brushed his fingers over the swoop of her neck and shoulder and she realized she was limited to caressing him through his dress shirt and pants. But the sundress she wore left her arms, most of her chest and her sensitive nape bare. He ran his finger slowly along the back of her neck.

"Am I your little lover boy?" he asked.

She groaned. "You know you are. I guess that makes me your sweet little baby?"

"Hell, yes. It makes you mine, Ace."

*His.*

She wanted to be his. She twined her arms around his neck and pulled his head to hers, dancing against him while they kissed. She sucked his tongue deep into her mouth and moved against him. Every nerve ending she had was so sensitized and ready for his touch. She was ready for this game to end. She wanted to touch his skin. Caressing his back through his shirt was fine, but she wanted the heat of his flesh. She wanted to see him instead of just remembering how muscly and firm he was under his clothing.

He pulled away then rested his forehead on hers as he looked down into her eyes. His hands still cupped her butt and he was swaying back and forth as "Texas Flood" started to play. The jazzy blues music continued to enflame her and the fact that it was this music, the music that had been the soundtrack to the start of their relationship, was making it hard for her to stay focused on the game she'd suggested they play.

Looking into Logan's blue eyes, she forgot everything. Everything but this man who she knew wasn't as perfect as he felt to her at this moment. At this moment, she had the feeling that they could make this work.

"I could do this all night," he said. "Just hold you in my arms and remember the past. When we were both young and it seemed like we could do whatever we wanted in life."

"Me too," she said, putting her hand on the side of his face. She felt the faint stubble there. She ran her finger over it, enjoying the roughness against the tip of her finger. "I'm sensing a but…"

"I want you, Ace. I like this, but I want to hold you naked in my arms, taste your hard nipples in my mouth, feel those bare limbs wrapped around me. I want that more than I want anything else."

The words were nothing more than the truth, and he knew he was a second away from shoving her skirt aside and cupping her naked ass. But he also didn't want to lose. He needed to make this last-ditch effort to get her to break first.

"I want that too. I love the feel of your naked chest rubbing against my breasts and the way your legs feel when they are tangled with mine as you drive up inside of me," she said.

He groaned and shook his head. She was on to him. "Not going to break first, are you?"

"Nope," she said with a grin.

A shot of something like love went through him. Quinn got to him in a way that no other woman ever had. God, he needed her. He needed more than he'd realized he did until this moment when her brown eyes were full of joy and desire.

She reached between them and he felt her hand wrap around his erection through his pants. He was already so hard that he knew it wasn't going to take much to push him over the edge. She ran her hand up and down his length and he tightened his muscles to keep from thrusting against her touch.

Logan tried to remember the rules she'd put in place but all he could think about was her naked and getting inside her. He lifted her off her feet and walked her back to the couch, sitting hard on the cushion. She bounced on his lap and he winced as he moved around, adjusting his legs and trying to make himself comfortable.

He reached for his zipper and drew it down, letting out a sigh of relief as he finally had room to get comfortable. She sighed too. Her fingers wrapped around him through the fabric of his briefs and stroked him. He lifted his hips and then reached his hand up under her skirt. Felt the smooth strength of her thighs and then the moistness at her center.

She shivered in his arms and then shifted until she was straddling him. She pushed his underwear down until his cock was free. He reached and made sure he was comfortable before she shifted around. He felt the heat of her center against him, the moist heat of her body rubbing against him, and knew that there were no losers in this moment.

He shifted his hips until the tip of his erection was at the entrance of her body. She put her hands on his shoulders and he cupped her naked butt.

Their eyes met and she pursed her lips. "Draw?"

"Draw," he said. He could live with that result as long as he didn't have to wait another second to get inside her.

Quinn lowered herself slowly onto him. She sucked her lower lip between her teeth as she took all of him and then paused, waiting for them both to adjust to him inside her. He drew his finger along her crack and felt her shiver in his arms, arching her back and thrusting her breasts forward as she let her head fall back.

He kissed her neck, suckled at that spot where her pulse beat strongly, and then urged her to start moving on him. She shifted backward, then thrust back down, riding him hard and taking everything he had to give. He was so close to the edge, so ready to come, that he couldn't wait another second. He reached between her legs, found that tiny bud, and rubbed it.

She pulled his head closer to hers, her mouth finding his as she rode him harder and faster. Then she ripped her mouth from his and cried out his name as she came, her hips moving more frantically against his. He rode the wave of her orgasm, driving up into her again and again until he came long and hard. She collapsed against him. He wrapped his arms around her and held her.

She had her head on his shoulder, her arms around his shoulders, and her breath brushed his neck each time she exhaled. He stroked her back up and down. Just holding her and hoping that this moment wouldn't end.

He'd never been the kind of man to hide from the world. But with Quinn in his arms and his life in tatters, he could easily stay here for the rest of his days and count himself content.

He knew that wasn't reality and that she'd have to go back to her job. That the real world was waiting for both of them. Dimly, he realized that Stevie Ray Vaughan was still playing from his smartphone. That music was so deeply ingrained in the soul of their relationship, he wondered if he'd been cheating at their game when he'd put it on.

"You okay?" she asked.

He glanced down, realizing she'd been watching him. Her brown eyes were fixed on him and he hoped she couldn't see the turmoil still swirling inside him. But this was Quinn, so she had probably already guessed it.

"Yeah," he said. What was one more lie from a Bisset? Apparently, that was something they were all very good at.

"Want me to stay the night?" she asked.

"If you want to," he said, trying not to seem vulnerable and ask her to stay. But he knew that he was vulnerable anyway.

Vulnerable to Quinn, who had always been able to see past all of his barriers to the heart of the man who always needed a win. The heart of a man who wanted her for himself and also wanted to beat her at the game they were always playing.

"I do."

# Fourteen

Waking up in Logan's arms was something she could get used to. It fit with where she was in her life to have a man, and Logan wasn't just any guy. He was the man she measured other men by, she realized.

He was the yard stick she'd always used. Most men didn't measure up. They weren't as driven, as fun, as sexy, as smart, as able to poke fun at themselves. And she'd never realized she'd been doing that until she was here with him and there was no comparison with other guys.

There was just Logan.

There always had been, which made her feel

scared and shaky. He wasn't a sure thing; he never had been. She'd taken a risk and she had to hope that he'd taken the same one. Last night, he'd needed her and she'd allowed herself to believe that it was the step toward building something together. And watching him sleep, seeing his face relaxed instead of tense, feeling his arms holding her to him, cuddling her to his side, it was easy to believe that this was the first morning of the rest of their lives.

If she allowed herself to forget that it was Logan Bisset, she could relax and just go with it.

But when had Logan ever done anything the easy way? He'd broken her heart once and she didn't want to believe she was the same woman who would fall for him again. But she knew she had. She could dress up however she wanted, say it was hot sex, or he needed her, and she liked that, but she knew deep down in her soul that she loved him.

Maybe...she always had.

She carefully rolled out of the bed and walked as quietly as she could to the bathroom, picking up her phone as she went. It was Saturday. Adler's wedding day.

She had a lot of work to do, and losing herself in her job was going to be a much-needed distraction. But another part of her, the part that she liked to bury deep inside—the romantic part—wanted Logan to wake up and beg her to stay.

She shook her head as she washed her face with

cold water. She needed to snap out of this. She had to get her head in the right place. A woman who wasn't on her A game couldn't compete with Logan. He liked the competition and as much as he loved to win, she knew he also loved the challenge.

And Quinn knew that Logan was never going to stop the game. Never going to take a break and let someone get the better of him. Even her. Even if he did care for her. She didn't need to get the better of him, she just wanted him. *Damn.*

She knew he cared for her. That was part of this. Part of why she'd fallen again. She could feel the emotions he had for her. Saw it in the way he'd wanted her to stay last night but had been reluctant to say it out loud. She gave him so many chances, but she had to, for herself. If she ever walked away, she'd always have some doubt that she'd left too soon.

This wasn't like college when they'd been young and still figuring out who they were going to be. They were in their thirties now and she was pretty damn sure of who she was. Still a hot mess on some days but killing it on others.

She reached for Logan's toothbrush and dug around in his overnight bag until she found his toothpaste. As she brushed her teeth, she tried to give herself a firm look in the mirror. It was hard to be serious when she was brushing her teeth. But she needed to be. If she ever needed to listen to that inner voice in her head, it was now.

This was Logan.

He hadn't magically changed into a domesticated man, he was still the driven alpha male he'd always been. He was wounded right now, which made him vulnerable and dangerous. It could go her way but, just as easily, she could end up hurt by him.

The way his mother had been last night.

Logan didn't pull punches and Quinn didn't want to be beat up by him. Not physically. He'd never lay a hand on her in anger, but he could rip her heart out if she let him.

How could she protect herself when her body and soul wanted him for her own? When she wanted to just open her arms and say that she was his.

Her phone pinged and she saw it was Adler. She was heading to the room they'd rented for the bridal party to get ready. The hair and makeup artists should be arriving soon.

Quinn typed out a response.

Hey. I'm at the hotel, need to run back to my place before I meet you. My assistant and the film crew will be there. You okay?

Nervous AF. Nick and I had it out last night. I think we are okay. Not sure.

What happened?

Just more Bisset BS. Also, if you want my advice, never fall in love with a guy.

You're not okay. Give me ten minutes or so and I'll meet you. Where are you?

Pulling into the hotel parking lot. Meet in the makeup room. There's nothing you can say to fix this.

That's not what I wanted for you today.

Me neither but that's where I am.

"You ever coming out, Ace?" Logan yelled through the closed door.

She rinsed, spit out the toothpaste, and went to open the door. He stood there totally naked and she just took a moment to appreciate how good he looked. He smiled at her and it felt genuine.

This was good. They were good. Everything was going to be okay, she thought.

"I have to run," she said. "Things are going to be busy today. But I'll see you at the wedding and then at the reception."

"Uh, I'm not going. I really don't want to be there."

Surprised she wrinkled her brow. "It's Adler's

day and she needs her family. You should go and so-cialize with everyone. It will make you feel better."

"Thanks, Quinn," Logan said sarcastically. "But I don't need your advice. I invited you up last night to screw not to be my shrink."

Quinn's face went white and then he saw her get pissed. He knew he was being an asshole. He shouldn't have said that to her but he wasn't going to just head down to the wedding like nothing had happened. Last night had been an oasis of calm in the middle of the craziness his life had become. But that was it. Nothing had been resolved and he'd slept for a few hours with Quinn in his arms, but most of the night his mind had been busy running through all the scenarios that would play out today.

He'd been cruel to his parents, he'd set in motion a business deal to ruin Nick's honeymoon, and his cousin probably would be happy if she didn't see him on her special day. Right now, he felt like the lowest of the low and he knew he deserved to feel that way.

Some of it, he placed on his mom's shoulders but since he'd stabbed her in the heart with his words last night, he knew that the blame had to come back to him. And the last thing he wanted was to wake up feeling like he did for Quinn.

He wasn't in any shape to be in a relationship with her, but no matter how he looked at it, they weren't just hooking up at the wedding. It felt like more.

And unless he missed his guess, she felt it too. He wondered if he shouldn't have played Stevie Ray Vaughan last night. Maybe bringing up the memories like that was why he'd woken up this morning feeling like…well, feeling. Just all the emotions. And Logan hated that. He was a man who prided himself on keeping his life together.

And emotional men made mistakes.

His dad was a prime example of that. A kid he didn't know about…hell, twins he hadn't known about.

He scrubbed his hand over his face. "What, no snappy comeback?"

"I'm waiting for an apology," she said. "That was uncalled for and we both know it."

"Keep waiting, Ace," he said.

She blinked and her jaw got tight. She took a deep breath through her nose and he knew that this time there'd be no getting back together with her. This time when Quinn walked out of his life, she wasn't coming back.

He'd had his second chance and once again he was going to let her go. It was the smart thing to do and God, please let him still be smart. He didn't know what he'd do if he lost that edge.

"Damn it, Logan. Every time I think you're anything more than a cold-blooded shark, you remind me that I'm wrong," she said.

"I never said this was anything more than you and me and the summer heat."

She shook her head. "The summer heat? Are you freaking kidding me?"

She turned on her heel and he watched her go, forced his eyes off her ass as she moved around his suite collecting her clothes and putting back on the dress she'd worn last night.

It was still crisp and pretty in the light of day. Her hair was tousled but she still looked good. And angry. Really angry.

"You cheated last night, so you think you won. You didn't," she said.

"Fine," he said. He didn't really want to talk about that anymore. He wanted her out of his room and out of his life so he could continue being himself. Stop trying to be the kind of man that Quinn would want by her side. Because he knew now that was what he'd been doing. Trying so hard to pretend that he could be a better man when he wasn't. He was just Logan Bisset.

And now he knew he didn't have any of Juliette Wallis-Bisset's genes. None of her kindness and charm. He was just the blunt businessman his father had raised him to be.

Quinn had all of her clothes back on and came toward him, barreling for the bathroom. He stepped back, not sure what she was going to do.

"I need my phone."

She reached the counter and took it before turning back to him. "I thought you felt lost and maybe you weren't sure who you were anymore now that you found out that Juliette isn't your mom. But that's not it, is it? You're still your dad's Mini-Me. Still the man who needs no one but himself and, hey, congrats, that's exactly what you're going to get from me and probably every other woman you have a relationship with."

Her words hurt and, as much as he knew he deserved them, they weren't the kind of words Quinn usually said to anyone. He'd hurt her that much that she was starting to be more like him. Cold, calculating. *Congratulations*, he thought, *you've made Quinn into a nasty person just like you*.

"I'd tell you I hope you'll be happy, but that's not really your thing, is it?" She didn't wait for an answer but just walked straight through the suite and out the door. And he stood there wondering if he'd made the biggest mistake of his life or not. He knew that Quinn would be happier without him and, as she'd pointed out, he was the kind of man who liked to be alone.

He'd be fine.

As he got ready to take a shower, he pretended that whatever else happened today, he was okay with her leaving the way she had. He almost convinced himself it was true too until he went to the balcony and saw her walking across the parking lot. Her steps were clipped and angry.

He knew that he was never going to be okay with how things ended. And he didn't deserve to be.

Adler took one look at her best friend's face and realized she'd been with a guy. It had to be Logan. He was the only man who had ever put Quinn off her stride. Of course, the man she'd have said had nothing in common with her fiancé except for their business acumen would be able to hurt Quinn deeply.

"Come on, let's talk," Adler said, looping her arm through Quinn's and dragging her to the second bedroom in the suite. She closed the door behind them, so they'd have some privacy.

Quinn wore a pair of black jeans and a black T-shirt under her silk bomber jacket. She was ready to work; she had her hair pulled back into a ponytail and hadn't bothered with makeup. Her creamy complexion complete with freckles made her seem younger than her age.

"Why didn't you say you were with Logan again?" Adler asked.

"How'd you find out?"

"You look ready to spit nails and like you've been crying. He's the only one I've ever known to affect you like that," Adler said. "Plus, given all the shit that's going on this weekend, it's logical."

"There's nothing logical about me and Logan. It's just hormones and stupidity."

Adler gave a shout of laughter before she shook her head. "What has he done?"

"Nothing. It's not important. You and Nick are fighting? That's what Mari texted Iris who texted me."

"You guys need a better way to communicate. That is so last night. Nick and I sort of made up."

"How do you sort of make up?" Quinn asked.

Adler was wondering the same thing herself, but Nick had come to her this morning and said that they shouldn't let the events of the last few days derail their wedding. He still wanted to marry her. But he hadn't said he'd loved her when she'd left and she couldn't help but wonder if he was going through the ceremony because he needed a distraction from the scandals swirling around him.

"We're getting married. We still haven't sorted everything out, but with the ceremony being televised and all the family stuff, we just have to go through with it."

Adler hated the way that sounded. She hadn't been looking to get married just to be a man's Mrs. She'd thought she'd found her soul mate and the man who'd be her partner through the rest of her life. That she'd made a better choice than her dad, who had taken a long time to find Sonia. But maybe she'd been a little too big for her britches by thinking that way.

"Oh, no, Ad, you guys are the perfect couple. I'm sure this is going to blow over."

She smiled at Quinn but could see on her friend's

face that she didn't believe it. Too much had happened for any of them to go back to where they had been before. She hoped that the wedding would be a step to her and Nick finding the way forward, but frankly he was drinking a lot and brooding. That wasn't the kind of man he'd been before. He was driven but he'd always been sort of open and upbeat, unlike the men in her family.

"No one is perfect," Adler said. "We're going to figure it out. What about you and Logan?"

Quinn shook her head. "There is no me and Logan. There's Logan, and he's pissed at the world. And there's me, who tried to make him see that this too shall pass."

Of course, Logan didn't want to hear that. Adler knew her cousin well enough to know he wouldn't be appeased by that. "He probably wants his pound of flesh."

"He got it last night. He said some really mean things to his mom and his dad," Quinn said. "I thought he was hurting and that he just needed some time— Never mind. You don't need to hear that."

"I'm sorry," Adler said. And she was. She wanted her friend to find happiness and the only man she'd been interested in seriously in a long time was Logan. There was something between the two of them that Adler didn't get, but that was love, wasn't it?

"Love is so weird. Aunt Jules still loves Auggie. Cora and Tad had their secrets and yet they are still together. Is it just the years keeping them united at this point or is some of it real emotions?" Adler asked. Once she'd believed that only the strong bond of love could keep a couple together, but now she didn't know. Who could love another person who kept those kinds of secrets?

"It is weird. And I'm not in love with Logan. I was in lust and I'm cured. What about you?"

"I'm still in love despite the fact that I'm ticked at Nick. He's the only man I want to be with. I guess that's why I'm going through with the wedding. I am upset, and he's unsure of himself right now, but I don't want to let him go. I still have hope that we can find our way back to each other."

Quinn gave her a sweet look and then hugged her. "I know you two will. You have to or else that means that the older generation and their machinations won. And that's not right. They were trying to hurt each other and you two are pure love and joy."

Adler shook her head. "I don't know about that, but I do know I'm not going to let their actions influence us any more than I have to. I'm going to marry Nick and we are going to start our life away from the craziness that is the Bisset-Williams feud."

"Good plan. Ready to start getting your hair and makeup done?"

"Yes. I want to do all the bride things and just get this day over with."

# Fifteen

Logan left the hotel and ended up at his grandmother Vivian's house. But after his behavior, he wasn't sure he'd be welcome there. At the last minute, he took a detour, starting down the path to the beach. He found himself sitting on the sand watching the waves when his brothers found him. Dare, Zac, Leo and… Nick. His half sibling—wait, his twin. The brother he didn't want to have.

"Thought we'd find you here," Dare said.

"Your powers of deduction are working overtime," Logan said sarcastically.

"Don't be more of an ass than you already have been," Leo said. "Adler texted Nick and told him that you and Quinn were a thing and you broke her heart. Again."

"Is that why you're here?" he asked. His brothers weren't the type to meddle in his affairs. They pretty much all kept the ups and downs of their love lives to themselves and he, for one, appreciated that.

"Yes and no," Dare said as he sat next to him. "I can't speak for the others, but I needed to get away from Mom and Dad and all the wedding stuff. No offense, Nick."

"None taken," Nick said, sitting next to Dare.

Zac walked to the water's edge, looked out at the horizon and then down at the beach, bending to pick up a shell. He used the incoming wave to wash the sand off it.

He walked back over to his brother, pocketing the shell as he did so. "I'm here to give you some advice, bro. I have no idea if you were just hooking up with Quinn or if you thought it was something else and the stuff with Mom and Dad threw you off. But if you have even the slightest feeling that she's the one, don't let her slip away. I have never felt worse than when I'd thought I'd lost Iris," he said.

"You were hung over," Logan pointed out.

Leo punched him in the shoulder. "Don't be a jerk. Do you feel like that for Quinn?"

He shrugged. This wasn't something he was going to discuss with them. "I don't know. Nick, can I have a moment of your time?"

He might not like Nick but the two of them had been fucked over a lot this weekend. And Logan didn't want to be responsible for another shock. He felt like it was only right to give his adversary a heads-up to what he'd done.

Nick arched an eyebrow at him and then nodded. "Sure. Alone?"

"Let's take a walk," Logan said, standing.

Nick fell into step beside him as they walked down the shore. Logan realized that he knew nothing about this man aside from his business practices and that they usually were going after the same prize.

"First of all, I'm not sure about the twin thing," Logan said. "I don't like you. I'm pretty sure you feel the same about me."

"You're not my favorite person," Nick said drolly. "But I appreciate you coming to the wedding for Adler's sake."

Logan shook his head. He was a grade-A asshole and it was time that Nick knew it. "I didn't come here for Adler. I did it because my mom—Juliette—told me that I would let the family down if I didn't come."

"Well, still you showed up," Nick said. "I'm not sure I would have."

*Fuck him.* "I had to get a little bit of myself back though. Couldn't give in and show up at your wedding and let you win."

Nick tipped his head to the side, a hard look coming over his face "Let me win? What did you do to get back at me?"

"I undercut you on the patent deal you've been working on and on Monday FuturGen is going to announce a new partnership with an LLC I own. That happened way before I learned any of this stuff about you being my twin."

Nick clenched his fists. "The patent? How did you even know I was interested in that?"

Logan wished the other man would punch him. God, he'd turned into the worst version of himself. Nick was getting married to Adler today. A better man would have— He cut himself off. He wasn't a better man.

"I have connections. Plus, I was watching the stocks you've been buying up," Logan said. "I'm sorry. I shouldn't have done it, but I'm August Bisset's son."

Nick nodded. "I get it. We've never been friendly."

"No, we haven't. But I am sorry. I don't know why I do things like that," he admitted. "I just can't stand to feel like I've lost. After the deal goes through I'll transfer the patent to you. I want it to be my wedding gift to you and Adler."

Nick nodded. "I used to be like that before Adler. But having her by my side, no one can best that. She…she makes me stronger than I am on my own."

"I doubt that," Logan said. Though he remembered Quinn pulling him from his parents before he'd made things worse last night.

"Maybe stronger is the wrong word. She makes me smarter. Now I normally think things through because I know that if I do the wrong thing…I'll lose her."

"Normally? Not this weekend, right? I mean, how could you handle this? I'm weirded out but it must be even worse for you."

"I don't know that it's worse for me than for you, but I'm struggling. My dad has been a rock. We always knew that I was someone else's son, just not that it was August. So Dad and I have a solid relationship."

He looked at the other man. Nick was taller than Logan and had dark hair where Logan was blond. He searched Nick's face trying to see something that would confirm they were twins, but there weren't really any physical signs. "That sounds nice. Normally, Dad and I are solid, but this whole thing with my mom…it's just pushed me over the edge. I said some shitty things to Quinn this morning. Like, even bad for me, and I know I should apologize but I can't figure out if that would be better for her."

Nick put his hand on Logan's shoulder and Logan looked at the other man, who had always been his enemy but somehow no longer was. "I've been screwing up left and right with Adler this entire weekend, but I do know that I will do anything to keep her by my side. There's not another woman in the world who I'd do that for. If you feel even close to that for Quinn, don't let her go."

Logan nodded. "Yeah, thanks. Aren't you afraid that what you feel for Adler is a liability? That she'll cause you to lose your edge?"

Nick stopped walking and put his hands on his hips as he turned to look at the ocean. "Without her I'd still be working sixteen-hour days and not have much of a life. Williams, Inc., is more profitable than it ever has been before and I have to say I think me being in a good place with Adler has a lot to do with it. Even your little stunt outmaneuvering me with the patent isn't going to really be a bad hit," Nick said with a wink before he turned and walked back toward his brothers. "I finally realized that there is more to living than work."

"Like what?"

"Having someone to share it all with."

Logan watched the other man—his twin—leave and thought about all he'd said. Quinn had always made him want to be a better man but there was a part of him that had resisted. Afraid to give up any of the things he'd believed made him who he was. But now that he was back to square one, why not remake himself as a better man? One who wanted Quinn by his side and could be the man she needed by hers.

"Make sure that we have cameras at the front of the church and that they are focused on the bride.

I'll use some of the drone footage for the guests and their reactions," Quinn said. "I know that everyone is tired. It's been a long day already and it's not even lunchtime. But we need to get this right."

"We will," her assistant said. "I've given the crew a forty-minute lunch break. The bride asked if you would join her and the bridesmaids off camera. She's in the suite still. The moms are…totally awkward. It's all frozen smiles and tension. But I think we can work around it. I'd hate to be the photographer for this gig."

"Me too," Quinn said. She bet it was awkward between Juliette and Cora. Both of them hadn't spoken since that day in the hospital when they'd made their deal and swapped babies.

She left the command center where her team was headquartered knowing Tillie had everything under control and went to find Adler. After their talk this morning, she was still ticked at Logan, but she'd pushed him to the back of her mind. He was in full-on corporate-jerk mode to her way of thinking. Knowing him, he wouldn't be at the wedding. In fact, she wouldn't be surprised if he had left Nantucket.

Her phone was quiet for once, which was a blessing, and she skimmed her social media feed as she walked to the elevator. She heard a familiar voice and glanced up to see Nick and Logan chatting with the other Bisset brothers. She took a moment, shaking her head. She would never have thought Logan could be civil to Nick. A lot had changed. But not enough.

She turned sharply into one of the staff hallways to avoid dealing with him.

Her heart hurt when she heard his voice, and she'd never been that good at hiding her feelings. In fact, the last time they'd broken up, she'd gone away for weeks to find herself again.

This shouldn't feel as intense as it did. It made her mad that she'd taken a chance on Logan and he'd been just…what? She really couldn't justify being mad at him for his actions. He'd never promised her anything. Never made it seem like he was hooking up with her to start a relationship.

It wasn't his fault that she'd fallen in love with him.

It was her own.

She should have known better than to think she could toy with Logan and not fall for him. But she hadn't. Also, he'd needed her. No matter what he might have said this morning, he'd needed her last night, and that had been the one thing that had driven her into his arms and lowered her guard.

Quinn took a deep breath. She wanted to believe she could be cool and that when she saw him again it wouldn't hurt. But love didn't work like that. And she was honest with herself, acknowledging she was always going to care for him no matter how he felt for her.

She had to figure out how to live with that. But not today. Today all she had to do was be Adler's friend and produce the best damned destination wedding episode that she could. And, honestly, she was happy to do that. Those things, in her wheelhouse, would give her something other than Logan to worry over.

She went back into the lobby; the men were gone, and she took the stairs up to the third floor where the suite Adler was using was located and knocked on the door.

Iris opened the door. Her friend was beaming. She'd been weathering the viral backlash from the news that she'd paid Zac to be her date this weekend and she and Zac had made up. As much as Quinn's own heart was aching, she was happy for Iris. Her friend deserved all the happiness she'd found when she'd fallen in love with Zac.

"About time you got here," Iris said. "Adler has something for us and she wouldn't let me have mine until you got here."

"Presents? I have something for her too, but it's downstairs."

"Same. Come on in. Are you any better? Adler told me what happened with Logan. I can't believe you…"

"Slept with him again, knowing he is love intolerant?"

Iris started laughing. "I wouldn't have put it that way, but yes."

"Me neither," Quinn said, looping her arm through Iris's as they made their way over to Adler.

"I'm so glad my besties are here," Adler said.

Quinn noticed that the room was empty except for the three of them. Adler was wearing a white robe embossed with her initials, as was Iris. The three of them went to sit on the love seat together.

"I got these for you…and okay, I got one for myself as well."

She handed them jewelry boxes. Quinn and Iris opened them and found Tiffany & Co. necklaces with the standard platinum heart charms. "I had no idea that I would be leaning on you two so hard this weekend. Thank you for having my back," Adler said.

Quinn turned the charm over and saw that it was engraved.

*Sisters of the Heart.*

Logan stood at the back of the church watching Adler and Nick's wedding. It changed something inside him, making him reexamine the thoughts that had been stirring in his head all day and forcing him to face hard truths about himself. Forcing him to face how he felt about Quinn. He saw her working; she'd pretty much ignored him except for one heartbreaking moment when he'd walked into the church by himself and their eyes had met.

He'd wanted to go to her and had started to but

she'd held her hand up and shaken her head before turning away. He'd seen the look on her face, known that she needed to work, and had left her to it. He hated to think that he was responsible for the dim light he'd seen in her eyes. But he knew he was.

His parents were seated in one of the front rows with Toby and his girlfriend. The Williamses were on the other side of the aisle. Cora Williams caught his eye, looking as if she wanted to talk to him, and Logan realized the woman was his biological mother. Looking at her, all he saw were the similarities between her and Nick. Was that why she'd given him up and kept Nick? Was it because Nick looked more like her? What a strange, irrational thing to think, but at the same time there it was.

But a few minutes after birth, would that have been obvious?

All the questions he had were swirling inside him again, but he glanced away and saw Quinn. Her back was to him. She wore a pretty, cream-colored dress that made her red hair and fair complexion even more eye-catching than normal. Just seeing her made him feel calmer. Better. He knew he loved her. He had been dancing around the thought since he'd woken alone in bed this morning. Hearing her in the bathroom, he'd thought about telling her. How happy he was to have her back in his life. Until the reality of his life had crashed around him.

He was trying to move forward. But how could

he when the past was right there stinging him every chance it got?

Somehow, the ceremony was over, and he didn't remember any of it except Nick and Adler walking out of the church. Nick had looked at him and tipped his head toward Adler as if to say, *This is what matters.*

Logan hung back, not sure if he should find his brothers or his parents. He just didn't feel like he fit in anywhere.

Cora came over to him by herself. "Do you have a minute to chat with me?" she asked. She had a quieter personality than his mom—than Juliette. She had thick black hair and kind blue eyes. His eyes, he realized.

"Um, sure. What did you want to talk about?"

She swallowed and then said, "Well, I imagine you have some questions for me."

Did he? Of course, he did. But this woman was the wife of one of his fiercest business rivals. Could he let himself be vulnerable in front of her? He knew he had to if he wanted to move past the feelings that were swirling inside him. "Why did you give me up?"

"I didn't pick Nick over you," she said. "You were the baby closer to Juliette and it was easier for us to swap you. I was so overwhelmed by having twins… there was a moment when I thought about giving both of you to her."

He didn't know what to say to that. Fate had given him to his mom—and he now acknowledged that Juliette was his mother, even if she hadn't given birth to him. There had been no rejection from Cora or choice on Juliette's part. Just fate pushing him to the family he needed to be raised in. "Thank you for telling me that. I… I don't know how we will go forward. I mean I'm pretty sure Tad isn't too pleased to hear that I'm related to you."

"He was surprised about August being the father. I had told him about having twins and the swap I'd made in the hospital," she said. "He's always hated August because of the way August cut him out of Bisset Industries, so I knew mentioning that I'd had an affair with August would…well, not be something he wanted to hear. And, honestly, I hadn't thought we'd see him at the wedding at all. Adler's not close to him."

"It was just the perfect storm," Logan said.

"Exactly. If you want to get to know me, I'd love that. And if you don't, that's fine too," she said. "I'm so happy to have the chance to get to see you as a man. I've thought of you often and hoped you'd ended up in a happy home."

"I did. I had a very good upbringing."

Cora reached out and hugged him. It was awkward at first because he was standing so stiffly. But he returned the embrace and heard her sigh.

He couldn't imagine what it had been like for her to live with the decision she'd made. "Thank you."

"You're welcome. It's the least I could do," Cora said.

The photographer was calling for the groom's parents and Cora smiled at him as she turned away. He watched her go. His life would have been different if he'd been raised by her and Tad, but he didn't know that it would have been better.

He saw his mom watching him and realized he owed her an apology. He started toward her and she motioned that she'd come to him.

"Mom, I'm so sorry for what I said last night," he said the moment she got to him.

Juliette pulled him close for a hug. "It's okay. I deserved it."

"No," he said firmly. "You didn't. I was being a jerk. I was raised better than I behaved, and I can only blame it…actually I have no excuse."

"You're a Bisset, Logan. No matter what, you react strongly to everything. Emotions are hard for you and I get that. You remind me a lot of your father," she said. "You always have. You're stubborn and brash."

"I am," Logan admitted. "Why have you stayed with him all these years?"

"Because he is always trying to be a better man. He loves me and I love him, and it's not easy, but each of these things we've lived through has brought us closer," she said.

"Mom, I could use your advice. I hurt Quinn and I need to win her back," he said. "Will you help me?"

"Yes, son," she said.

# Sixteen

His brothers drifted over to them in the back of the church. Zac was at the front with the bridal party, but Leo and Dare were with him. Mari had gone outside to take a call from Inigo. And his dad was nowhere to be seen.

"You know it's not that your father and I ignore the mistakes, we just try to find a way to use them to make us stronger as a couple. I hope you boys know that," his mother said.

"I don't necessarily understand it, but it seems to work for you two," Logan said.

"It does," Dare added, and Leo nodded.

"What works?" August said as he came up behind them. "Did you two have your talk, Logan?"

"Yes, sir. I already apologized to Mom for my behavior last night, but I owe you one as well," he said as he turned to face his father.

His dad clapped him on the shoulder. "Apology accepted. I would have said something similar in your shoes. I am sorry that my past actions have caused so much strife for you lately. I hope you know that I have never regretted being your father. No matter the circumstances of your birth, I've always loved you."

"I know, Dad," he said. "I love you and Mom too."

"Damned straight. You got the best parents," he said.

"I wouldn't go that far," Dare said. "You do have exacting standards."

"Which has served you well in your political career," August said. "As a matter of fact, I have a lobbyist I want you to talk to. Got a minute?"

"Sure," Dare said.

"I'm going to check on Adler. I feel so bad that her mother's not here to share this special moment, and that my actions caused her extra stress," his mom said. "It was a beautiful ceremony though."

"It was," Logan agreed as his mom walked away.

"There's Danni," Leo said.

Logan saw the woman Leo had been unsuccessfully trying to woo all weekend. "Go and see if you can work your magic today."

"I pretty much have no game with her, Logan. I'm not sure why."

"Because you're not the player you think you are. Stop trying to front, and be yourself," he said.

"Myself?"

"Yeah. It will work a lot better than whatever you've been doing," he said.

Leo nodded and then walked away. Logan realized how lucky he was to be a part of his family. He had thought that learning about his true biological mother had changed him but, fundamentally, it hadn't. He was still the man he'd always been. But he could be better. He'd been working toward being a better man from the moment he'd seen Quinn again.

At the bonfire.

When he'd realized that he wanted her. He'd sold it to himself as a distraction because that had been easier to handle at that moment, but he knew it had never been that. One look and he'd started to fall for her again.

He'd regretted losing her, and she'd be the first to point out that was because he couldn't stand not winning, but the truth was, he hadn't meant to hurt her or to let her leave once much less twice.

He'd always believed he was stronger on his own, but his parents had proven that wasn't the case. Even Nick had said he thought having Adler by his side had given him an edge in business.

Quinn could do that for him. She was already

showing him that he could have a life away from work. That there were other parts of his life that he couldn't keep ignoring. Watching Adler and Nick pose together and seeing Quinn off to the side watching them, Logan knew what he had to do.

He walked over to her. She shook her head, but he came closer. "I need to talk to you. Can you take a break for a few minutes?"

"Please don't do this right now. I'm trying to work," she said.

"I can wait. Just tell me when."

"When?" she asked. "How about never?"

"That won't do," he said.

She grabbed his wrist and turned, pulling him to the back of the church and out the door. They faced off in the deserted parking lot; the guests had gone on to the reception and the bridal party and family were inside.

"What are you doing?" she asked. "I'm not ready to be chill and just say yeah, everything's cool. And you seem like you just want some closure so you can move on. I can't do that. Not today."

He shook his head. "I know that. I was a jerk earlier and I have no excuse except that I didn't know how to tell you that I'm falling in love with you. That I wanted you to stay with me and I knew I had no right to ask. Everything felt like it was shifting, that my world was turning into something new."

She put her hand on his jaw. "Oh, Logan. I know

that. I get that you're not yourself right now. But I expected you to treat me with respect. I can't be with a man who doesn't understand that."

Logan nodded. He'd hurt her in a way she wasn't going to just forgive, and he didn't blame her. He was going to have to show her he'd changed and that was going to take more time than he had this afternoon.

"I'm sorry, Ace. I wish I'd never said those things, but you know the man I am. I can't even promise that I'd never behave that way again. But I will tell you that I will keep trying to change and to show you how much you mean to me."

She shook her head. "Don't. Don't make rash statements like that."

"Why?"

"I might believe them and I'm not sure that I should. In fact, I know I shouldn't because you're not the kind of man who is capable of that kind of gesture."

Logan was saying all the right things and Quinn wanted to believe him. She loved him, so that made her see him in the way her heart wanted her to. But her mind wasn't having it. Just this morning he'd turned from the sexy lover of the night before into a man who'd cut her to ribbons. She didn't want to be the kind of woman who ended up in a relationship like that. As much as it hurt to say no, she knew she had to. Because if he hurt her again, she wouldn't be able to forgive him or herself.

"Fair enough," he said. "I don't really deserve a second chance from you, but would you consider giving me some time to prove I'm not the man you think I am? That I have changed for the better?"

"How would you do that? I live in California and Bisset Industries is here on the East Coast. I think it's best if we both just walk away. Take this as a little P.S. from our affair in college and leave it there."

He watched her with an inscrutable expression on his face. His jaw clenched and his hands moved restlessly at his sides, as if he wanted to touch her but didn't trust himself.

"I can't do that. I'm my best self when I'm with you. And this morning was a lifetime ago. I had to come to terms with all of the changes in my life, and I'm not going to lie and tell you that I'm one hundred percent there yet. But losing you, watching you walk out, woke me. Showed me that I don't want a life without you, Quinn. I know it's asking a lot of you, and I don't expect to change your mind. But I have to try. I've never felt this way about anyone before. I love you."

She shook her head. "That's not fair. You can't say that. Not now. I told you—"

"That you'll believe me? I hope you do. Because I'm not a man to lie to anyone. You know that about me. I'm not saying this because I think it will make you come back, I'm saying it because it's true. Whether you let me back into your life or not, my feelings for you won't change. Love doesn't work that way. And it took losing you for me to understand that."

She was struggling to keep her guard up, to keep the walls in place. But this was Logan. He had never been the kind of man to not speak his truth. He'd never been someone to use falsehoods to woo her. He'd been honest from the beginning.

"I want to believe you."

"That's a start," he said. "Will you take a chance on me? Let me prove to you that this morning was just me reacting badly to events I couldn't control."

Torn, she could just stare at him.

His expression changed and he sighed. "I don't blame you if you say no."

*Say no.*

Could she live with herself if she did? She'd always regret it if she didn't give him a chance. She wanted a chance too. With Logan. The man she loved.

He took her hand in his. "Please."

She stared into his bright blue eyes, not sure she'd heard him right.

"I'm begging you to give me another chance," he said. "I don't want to live the rest of my life knowing that I let you get away—twice."

"Is this because you feel like, if I do, you won't

win?" she asked. She had to ask. He hated losing so much, he'd undercut Nick to prove that he wasn't giving in to a Williams.

"No. It's not because I want to put a tick mark in the win column. I need you with me because I love you. You make life fun and exciting. You make me engage in things when I'd rather just sit and sulk. My life is so much better with you in it. I love you."

"I love you too," she admitted.

Her assistant came out, followed by the rest of the bridal party, and Logan moved so that he was standing between her and them. "I know you have to work but I can't leave it like that. Will you give me a second chance? Can we be a couple?"

"Yes," she said.

He pulled her into his arms and kissed her long and deep. There was the sound of applause, but she could only hear Logan whispering in her ear how much he loved her and how lucky he was to have her by his side.

She went back to work, finishing up filming a few more church shots, and Logan just waited for her. She knew that his life wasn't always going to enable him to wait on her while she was working, but she appreciated that he had.

They went to the reception hand in hand. He stopped before they walked inside.

"I don't know if I can always be perfect," he said.

"I know you can't be, Logan. That's part of what I

love about you. As long as we're partners and you're not trying to compete with me, we can make this work."

"We can. I want that more than anything," he said. "I love you, Ace."

"I love you too," she said.

Adler came out of the hall by herself, tears streaming down her face.

"What's the matter?"

"Auggie and Tad are fighting. Nick punched Auggie in the eye."

Logan ran into the rehearsal hall and Quinn and Adler followed. The two older men were having a standoff and Nick was between them. Logan raced to their sides, standing by Nick. He looked over at Quinn and Adler and then nodded.

"You two are going to have to figure out a way to get along. Nick and I are twins, Dad. You're now related to each other by Adler's marriage. The rivalry has to end or you are going to both lose everything."

* * * * *

# WE HOPE YOU ENJOYED
## THIS BOOK FROM

### HARLEQUIN
# DESIRE

*Luxury, scandal, desire—welcome to*
*the lives of the American elite.*

Be transported to the worlds of oil barons, family dynasties, moguls and celebrities. Get ready for juicy plot twists, delicious sensuality and intriguing scandal.

**6 NEW BOOKS AVAILABLE EVERY MONTH!**

## COMING NEXT MONTH FROM

# DESIRE

### #2863 WHAT HAPPENS ON VACATION...

*Westmoreland Legacy: The Outlaws* • by Brenda Jackson

Alaskan senator Jessup Outlaw needs an escape...and he finds just the right one on his Napa Valley vacation: actress Paige Novak. What starts as a fling soon gets serious, but a familiar face from Paige's past may ruin everything...

### #2864 THE RANCHER'S RECKONING

*Texas Cattleman's Club: Fathers and Sons* • by Joanne Rock

Pursuing the story of a lifetime, reporter Sierra Morgan reunites a lost baby with his father, rancher Colt Black. He's claiming his heir but needs Sierra's help as a live-in nanny. Will this temporary arrangement withstand the sparks and secrets between them?

### #2865 WRONG BROTHER, RIGHT KISS

*Dynasties: DNA Dilemma* • by Joss Wood

As his brother's ex-wife, Tinsley Ryder-White is off-limits to Cody Gallant. Until one unexpected night of passion after a New Year's kiss leaves them reeling...and keeping their distance until forced to work together. Can they ignore the attraction that threatens their careers and hearts?

### #2866 THE ONE FROM THE WEDDING

*Destination Wedding* • by Katherine Garbera

Jewelry designer Danni Eldridge didn't expect to see Leo Bisset at this destination-wedding weekend. The CEO once undermined her work; now she'll take him down a peg. But one hot night changes everything—until they realize they're competing for the same lucrative business contract.

### #2867 PLAYING BY THE MARRIAGE RULES

by Fiona Brand

To secure his inheritance, oil heir Damon Wyatt needs to marry by midnight. But when his convenient bride never arrives, he's forced to cut a marriage deal with wedding planner Jenna Beaumont, his ex. Will this fake marriage resurrect real attraction?

### #2868 OUT OF THE FRIEND ZONE

*LA Women* • by Sheri WhiteFeather

Reconnecting at a high school reunion, screenwriter Bailey Mitchell and tech giant Wade Butler can't believe how far they've come and how much they've missed one another. Soon they begin a passionate romance, one that might be derailed by a long-held secret...

---

**YOU CAN FIND MORE INFORMATION ON UPCOMING HARLEQUIN TITLES, FREE EXCERPTS AND MORE AT HARLEQUIN.COM.**

HDCNM0222

The ranch was more than a birthright—it was the thing that made him a Hartmann. His dad made him promise. Maybe Nick couldn't voice why that promise was important to him. Why he cared. His brothers shrugged the responsibility so easily, but he was shackled by it. His legacy couldn't be losing the thing that had made him. No. He couldn't fail at this. Not even to be with her, the mermaid incarnate.

She smiled her odd half smile and splashed some water at him again. "I don't think you even know all you want, cowboy." She bit her lip, drawing his attention instantly to the one thing he'd wanted since meeting her at the airport. He followed her in a second lap of the pool, catching up to her in the deep end.

"So your brother married your prom date?" She widened her eyes as she issued her question.

"It was a long time ago." He cleared his throat. Maybe Ben was right and he needed to open up a bit.

"Yes, you're practically ancient, aren't you?" She swatted a bit of water in his direction, which he managed to sidestep.

"Careful, Oxford." He smiled, unable to help himself. It felt good to smile, even more so when faced with the crushing sadness he'd been shouldering for the past three weeks.

"Can you not call me that?" She paused. "My sister went to Oxford. And I don't want to think about her right now."

Her bottom lip jutted forward and quivered. It provoked a response he was unprepared for, and he sealed her concern with a kiss so thorough it rocked him.

Everything he wanted to say he said with the kiss. *I'm sorry. I want you. I'm hurting. Let's forget this.* Her body, hot against his, was a welcome heat to balance the chill of the pool. It was soft and deliciously curved. The perfect answer to his desperate question.

His tongue parried hers and she opened to him with an earnestness that rocked him. A soft mew of submission and he lifted her legs around his, arousal pressed plainly against her. She wrapped her legs around him, the thin skin of the bathing suit a poor barrier, and bit gently at his lip.

"I'm sorry," he started.

"Let's not be sorry, not now." Gone was the sorrow. Instead, she looked at him with a burning fire that he matched with his own.

*Don't miss what happens next in*
Montana Legacy
*by Katie Frey.*

*Available April 2022 wherever*
*Harlequin Desire books and ebooks are sold.*

Harlequin.com

# Get 4 FREE REWARDS!

**We'll send you 2 FREE Books plus 2 FREE Mystery Gifts.**

FREE Value Over $20

Both the **Harlequin® Desire** and **Harlequin Presents®** series feature compelling novels filled with passion, sensuality and intriguing scandals.

---

**YES!** Please send me 2 FREE novels from the Harlequin Desire or Harlequin Presents series and my 2 FREE gifts (gifts are worth about $10 retail). After receiving them, if I don't wish to receive any more books, I can return the shipping statement marked "cancel." If I don't cancel, I will receive 6 brand-new Harlequin Presents Larger-Print books every month and be billed just $5.80 each in the U.S. or $5.99 each in Canada, a savings of at least 11% off the cover price or 6 Harlequin Desire books every month and be billed just $4.55 each in the U.S. or $5.24 each in Canada, a savings of at least 13% off the cover price. It's quite a bargain! Shipping and handling is just 50¢ per book in the U.S. and $1.25 per book in Canada.* I understand that accepting the 2 free books and gifts places me under no obligation to buy anything. I can always return a shipment and cancel at any time. The free books and gifts are mine to keep no matter what I decide.

Choose one: ☐ **Harlequin Desire**
(225/326 HDN GNND)

☐ **Harlequin Presents Larger-Print**
(176/376 HDN GNWY)

_____
Name (please print)

_____
Address                                                      Apt. #

_____
City                          State/Province          Zip/Postal Code

**Email:** Please check this box ☐ if you would like to receive newsletters and promotional emails from Harlequin Enterprises ULC and its affiliates. You can unsubscribe anytime.

> **Mail to the Harlequin Reader Service:**
> **IN U.S.A.:** P.O. Box 1341, Buffalo, NY 14240-8531
> **IN CANADA:** P.O. Box 603, Fort Erie, Ontario L2A 5X3

Want to try 2 free books from another series? Call 1-800-873-8635 or visit www.ReaderService.com.

---

*Terms and prices subject to change without notice. Prices do not include sales taxes, which will be charged (if applicable) based on your state or country of residence. Canadian residents will be charged applicable taxes. Offer not valid in Quebec. This offer is limited to one order per household. Books received may not be as shown. Not valid for current subscribers to the Harlequin Presents or Harlequin Desire series. All orders subject to approval. Credit or debit balances in a customer's account(s) may be offset by any other outstanding balance owed by or to the customer. Please allow 4 to 6 weeks for delivery. Offer available while quantities last.

**Your Privacy**—Your information is being collected by Harlequin Enterprises ULC, operating as Harlequin Reader Service. For a complete summary of the information we collect, how we use this information and to whom it is disclosed, please visit our privacy notice located at corporate.harlequin.com/privacy-notice. From time to time we may also exchange your personal information with reputable third parties. If you wish to opt out of this sharing of your personal information, please visit readerservice.com/consumerschoice or call 1-800-873-8635. **Notice to California Residents**—Under California law, you have specific rights to control and access your data. For more information on these rights and how to exercise them, visit corporate.harlequin.com/california-privacy.

HDHP22